"You Can't Eat Flowers"

By

Linda Hewett

Published by New Generation Publishing in 2020

Copyright © Linda Hewett 2020

First Edition

The author asserts the moral right under the Copyright, Designs and Patents Act 1988 to be identified as the author of this work.

All Rights reserved. No part of this publication may be reproduced, stored in a retrieval system or transmitted, in any form or by any means without the prior consent of the author, nor be otherwise circulated in any form of binding or cover other than that which it is published and without a similar condition being imposed on the subsequent purchaser.

ISBN 978-1-80031-818-2

www.newgeneration-publishing.com

"No-one has ever lived in the past. Everyone has always lived in now – being alive in the past felt the same as being alive now – it was just a different version of today."

Chris Wild, www.retronaut.com – *The Photographic Time Machine*

Before we begin ...

Some say I have a vivid imagination. That's true, but I never imagined I would ever write a novel. Poems, short stories, articles – yes, I was in my comfort zone with those – until one wet, windy autumn day when I was searching for my next writing project.

I was watching the rain sweep across my garden when it came to me – if you're looking for the solution to a problem, you'll often find it 'right in front of your nose'.

I live in a converted Victorian workhouse. Yes, I know. Sounds a bit odd, but it's not, it's fascinating. The old buildings have been transformed into a courtyard of charming cottages, known in Hursley village as 'The Square', and I'm lucky enough to live in one of them, with my cat Maisie.

Over the years I'd thought about those 'inmates', wondering what their lives might have been like, but had never taken any steps to find out – that is until that rainy day when I started Googling the subject. Within a minute or two, or so it felt, I was hooked.

Before leaving my writing 'den', I looked out of the rain streaked window, and there she was, walking across what would have been the workhouse yard ...

The inspiration for my next writing project was here, 'right in front of my nose'.

Ellen
August 1911

Do you believe in the unbelievable?

You don't?

Perhaps you'll think again when you reach the end of my tale.

When it begins, I'm at my wit's end, filled with dread for the future of my family.

Every moment of the unimaginable events that follow remains etched in my mind, after more than thirty years. In my dreams I relive it all, still humbled that she chose to visit me when our fate was sealed ... or so we believed.

Chapter 1

The worst has happened

Ellen
August 1880

I know it.

The instant I hear Mother stumbling down the stairs.

I keep my eyes tight shut; if I open them, her tear-streaked face will tell me everything – everything we've been dreading. My eyes overflow as we hug. She sobs as if she'll never stop.

She stammers, "My poor Albert … on our bed upstairs … never able to take another breath …"

I clutch her close.

"My loving husband, worked hard all his life … always put the family's needs before his own …" She fights to hold back her bitter tears. "He's been taken from us."

Father's illness had started with a simple cough – which we thought was nothing to fear – but he was quickly confined to bed. Mother could barely hold up her head in the village when she found she couldn't afford the money for a doctor.

And now, after only two weeks, he's dead.

This is more than cruel …

She clings on to me, as if she can never let me go. "The best husband and father anyone could wish for. Whatever are we going to do without him?"

How I wish I had the answer. What *will* we do without him? I'm as heartbroken as she is.

She wrings her hands. "Albert was our tower of strength; we all loved him and relied on him. He gave us his love, his care and protection."

She barely manages to whisper the questions I've been trying not to think about.

"How will we find enough money to pay for the funeral? And we'll have to leave this cottage, and start paying rent, once a new head gardener is found."

Mother and I make a modest living as laundresses in the village, and there's my Joe's labourer's wage as well, but without Father's considerable earnings on the estate we'll be left with small fry, barely enough to keep the family.

She covers her face with her hands. "And now I'll have to dye some clothes to wear for mourning ..."

I don't know what to say.

Upstairs, I stand next to the bed, my heart pounding as I gaze down at my poor, dead father while Mother busies herself drawing the curtains and covering the mirror. Finally, we stand together, holding hands, battling to hold down our sobs.

I try to reassure her. "Try not to worry, Mother. It'll be hard for all of us, but we'll do our very best to manage – it's what Father would expect, and you know Joe and I will do everything we can to help you."

I daren't think about how much more work there'll be for all of us, now Father's gone.

*

The next week passes by in a haze of overwhelming grief, with Father's body resting in its coffin in the parlour, ready for the funeral we can hardly afford.

Sleepless nights are filled with heart-rending sobs from our poor boys, despite my soothing cuddles and comforting words.

Joe is as distressed as I am. Father had been a great support to him, always encouraging him in his farm-labouring tasks. He looks after Nellie, our family's pig – I've even seen him give her a cuddle when he thinks I'm not looking – and he takes charge of the chickens, with James and Henry helping, always making time to feed them and collect the eggs at the end of his long days on the farm.

But now he'll have much more on his plate. Where will he find the time?

*

I try – but fail – not to let the family see me in the worst of my grief. We're all struggling, and in truth, each of us gives in to more than our fair share of crying. No one has much of an appetite, but Mother persuades us to try some tiny portions, which we do, to please her.

And it's not only our family and neighbours who are grieving: the staff up at the estate are sharing our sadness. Two of Father's under gardeners, Sam and Tom, wearing black hat bands and gloves, arrive to offer their condolences on behalf of all the gardeners. Mother invites them in and puts the kettle on the fire for some tea.

Tom's face is forlorn. "Mrs Freeborn. We are all *so* sorry for your loss."

Hearing these words, Mother succumbs to her tears, despite her best efforts not to.

He continues, "Head gardeners like Mr Freeborn are hard to come by; it won't be an easy task for the squire to replace him."

Sam joins in, trying to hide his wet eyes, "We were fortunate indeed, Mrs Freeborn, to learn our trade under his guidance. He was a well-respected, hardworking man."

Tom has some unexpected news. "The squire has asked me to let you know he has organised a collection, to help with the funeral expenses."

"Oh, Tom …" She closes her eyes. "Please convey my heartfelt thanks to him. He's such an honourable man." Her tea goes cold.

*

"I think it's time for our evening walk, my love. The fresh

air will do us good."

It's three long weeks since our loss, and the funeral is at last behind us. We are all still suffering from lack of sleep. Joe and I have started taking a short walk across the fields at the end of our working day, while Mother stays at home with the boys. We need some time away from the house, with its sadness, just for a little while, and our walk helps us to cope.

We stand amongst the gleanings, at the edge of a field of corn that Joe helped to harvest, the setting sun lavishing its welcome warmth upon us. How heavenly he smells: of fertile soil, cornstalks and lush grass. We shield our eyes against the brightness, hoping to catch a glimpse of the skylarks, high in the late summer sky, singing solely for us.

But something's the matter. I can tell from the way he clutches hold of my hand: tightly rather than gently. He isn't the same man this evening, the warm, smiley, attentive Joe I married.

A stab of fear pains me as I twist my wedding ring, around and around.

His eyes take on a serious look. "I'm sorry to do this on such a fair evening love, I don't want to spoil our walk, but there's something I must tell you. I thought it best to wait until we were out here, on our own."

Fretful butterflies flutter in my chest.

He begins, "This is so hard for me –" he tries to give me a hug, but I turn away. Surely, we've had enough bad news, I don't want to deal with any more.

His voice is chilling. "It comes to something when a husband can no longer provide for his family."

I stare up into his face. "What do you mean, you can no longer provide for us?" I can hear the despair in his voice. I shudder.

He stiffens his shoulders and no longer wants to meet my eyes. What is it he hasn't told me? Is it the gossip I've heard in the village? About problems on the farms?

I blurt out, "Joe! Tell me! Surely *your* job isn't in danger?"

This can't be happening to my lovely Joe. He'd be the last labourer ever to be laid off. I've heard it said by many that he's one of the best, always more than meeting every farmer's needs; a valuable employee indeed, not one to let go for no good reason.

I stare at him as he continues. "I'm so sorry, love, but just as I'd feared, Mr Jacobs has told me I'll be laid off at the end of the week."

I don't know what to do with myself. This is more than I can cope with, on top of everything else.

My temper takes control. "This is the worst possible time you could choose to tell me such dreadful news! How on earth will Mother and I make ends meet and feed us, not only without Father's income, but now," I spit out the words, "without *yours*?"

He knows, as well as I do, what happens to folk who, through no fault of their own, become paupers.

I screw up my hands into a cold ball. "If we don't have enough money to manage, we'll have no choice but to …" If I don't say it, it won't happen.

"Yes, love, I know. But it won't come to that. I won't give up. I'll search and search until …" His distress makes it hard for him to continue. His cheeks are pale. "If there was any other way, love … but there isn't. I'm ashamed of myself for letting you all down; you know it's the last thing I want to do. But whichever farm I visit, they tell me the same story: they're at their wits end. Bad harvest follows bad harvest, and they have to lay off their *current* workers, certainly not take on new ones. They have no choice."

He pauses, wan-faced, trying to stand tall before he goes on. "The bald fact is this: we labourers can't begin to compete with these wretched threshing machines. Just *one machine* can do the work of many men – and now, if that isn't enough, steam tractors are taking over much of the work in the fields. We simply can't match what they can do."

I grip his hand. Can my heart sink any lower?

I move away to gaze across the familiar fields, to take a calming breath, trying to blot out his words.

But he hasn't finished. "It's no good, love, we have to face up to it: there'll be no new work for the likes of me hereabouts. I'm not surprised, I could see it coming, but I didn't want to worry you, so I kept it to myself until I'd spoken to Mr Jacobs."

"And now you know for sure." My heart aches. And so does his.

"I've already started doing the rounds, cap in hand, pleading with the local farmers, but it's the same story everywhere. They'd *like* to take me on, with all my experience, but they have to turn me away. I'm afraid I'll have to leave you all behind, and search for work much further afield."

This is more than hard to hear. It will change all our lives, of this there's no doubt.

I'm fiddling with my ring again and my tears overflow, thinking about the boys. "And what about James and Henry? They'll think you're *choosing* to leave them. They've only just lost their grandfather, now they'll be afraid they'll never see their father again, either. Their lives won't be the same without you: they *need* their father to be *here*."

I sink down on the stubbly field path. "And how are Mother and I going to manage everything on our own? You're so good with the chickens and with Nellie, no one could look after them better than you. You plant the allotment, prune the apple tree, chop the logs – the list is endless. You do so much for us. You're our rock, you know that."

I'm at the end of my tether.

Eventually, after an uneasy silence, I drive my anger away, knowing it isn't helping either of us, ashamed of myself for giving in to it. Instead, I take hold of his hand, and nuzzle my tear-streaked face into his neck, feeling the strong beat of his heart. Whatever happens, I'll always love him dearly.

I know this is not what he wants. We must trust that he *will* find another job to help provide for us. I have every faith in him, and I pray fervently for the day when the boys will have their father living at home once more, bringing us his wages, and more importantly, his love.

Hand in hand we stumble home, unable to console one another.

I must face up to it: my hard-working husband, loving father to Henry and James, is facing unemployment. He must take on a daunting, soul-destroying search for work, and he could end up miles away from us for weeks on end.

And he might return with none.

Chapter 2

What's the point of *me?*

Susie
August 2019

Thank you for taking the time to read my story – it's rare for me to tell it – to describe the whole sequence of extraordinary events. When I try, my friends don't believe me; they say it sounds like fiction, a product of my wild imagination; which is why it's so reassuring that you've chosen to read it.

After everything that happened, I've learnt an important lesson about life: truth is often stranger than fiction.

*

Susie
September 2018

No warning.

Simply another humdrum day stretching ahead, filled with any obsessive, repetitive cleaning task. I'm soon engrossed in dusting my houseplants, from which there isn't a mote of dust to remove.

And I know.

I know it's time to stop pretending: I must face up to the appalling person I've become.

I press my nails into my palms.

Hard.

Where has the care-free, giggly, sociable Susie disappeared to? The Susie who cared about every child she taught, enjoyed a glass of prosecco with friends, and was addicted to crime fiction. Is she lost, never to be found?

I can't lie to myself any longer. The bald truth is this: I've turned into a drab, unkempt, middle-aged woman; pale, dull-eyed, with unwashed hair, constantly clutching a new yellow, too-clean duster. She's no stranger – in fact I know her better than I know anyone else. Why have I denied it for so long? Because the woman is me.

And I hate her.

I instinctively close my eyes and bite my lip until my whole mouth tastes of blood. Every day these eyes tell me the truth. They show me exactly who I am. Now I close them tight and cover them with my hands, willing the repellent image I see every single day to fade.

I let the duster drop to the highly polished wooden floor and I slide slowly down the wall to the ground.

I shudder, and howl out these words for my pitiful self to hear, "What's the point of my life? What's the point of *me*?"

My sobs get louder and louder, until I manage to struggle to my feet, to rage out into the room, where no one is listening.

Finally, bone-weary, I slip to the floor again, to mop my face with the ridiculous, redundant yellow duster, and cradle my pounding head in my hands.

I'm beside myself. Exhausted from over-thinking, I dredge my mind for a way through, to stop lying to myself and papering over the cracks.

And there I stay, red-eyed, listening to the echoes of my question, longing for a liberator.

But no one comes.

*

"We can be perfectly happy without a baby." This has always been Steve's mantra. "A child would only complicate things. We're fine. Let's stay as we are."

But I don't want to '*stay as we are*'.

I'm nearly forty years old when I get pregnant. I knew

I'd have far less chance of conceiving a child as I got older, and I'd persuaded myself that I wouldn't care one way or another, so I'm surprised and secretly delighted by the joy that washes over me when the pregnancy test shows good news. I tell myself that Steve will soon get used to the idea and a baby might help bring us closer again.

Really? What planet am I on?

Lying to myself has become a habit … one that needs to be broken.

*

I wait to break the news until the evening, after dinner, when he's enjoying a couple of lagers, hoping against hope that now the pregnancy is *real*, his protest won't be so harsh.

"No wine for you tonight, Susie?"

"No … and not for a while …"

He stares at me, frowning. "That's not like you! Whatever's brought this on? You love your Prosecco!"

I move closer to catch hold of his hand. "I've got some news."

An uneasy silence.

I don't want to hide it, and there's no point in trying to sugar coat it.

I say it straight. "We're … going to have a baby!"

He flings my hand away and stands up, knocking the kitchen chair over, his face grim.

I try to catch hold of his hand again. "I only found out today … and I'm so excited!"

I pause, forcing a smile, ready for the tirade that I hope – in vain – won't arrive.

"So that's it then." He stares out of the window, at nothing in particular, his back to me. "Our lives are going to change *forever.*"

He raises his voice. "And I thought you were taking the pill! You always said you understood how I felt about having a child."

He heads for the kitchen door. "Sorry, I need some space to get my head round this. In all our discussions about having a baby you said you knew it was unlikely to happen at our age anyway, and you were okay with that." Sadness softens his tone. "And you know my feelings about … knowing how to be a good dad."

I almost feel sorry for him as I watch him escape upstairs. He's quite right of course – I know he's never been keen on us having children, no point in denying it.

I also couldn't deny that I haven't been taking the pill.

Without telling him.

*

I'll never forget the day he told me all about it, when we were first engaged. It came as a surprise – it didn't fit with my image of him. We'd enjoyed our usual Sunday lunch at our favourite pub and were waiting for our coffee to arrive.

He struggled to raise the subject. "Susie, I need to ask you – sorry, but this is hard for me – I need to know how you feel about … us having children. We haven't really talked about it, have we, but we should, don't you think, now we're going to be married?"

I reached out my hand across the table, "Yes, of course we can talk about it, but I suppose I naïvely thought that having a child would just *happen*; I didn't see it as an issue that could become a problem between us. Why? Are you worried about it?"

He fiddled with his paper napkin. "The thing is – and I know this is going to sound strange – but I'm sure, in fact I know for certain, that I wouldn't make a good father."

He didn't look at me.

I frowned. "Really? Why on earth not?"

"Well …" He squirmed in his chair. My eyes widened as he said, "The thing is – I never met my *own* dad."

Oh, my goodness. I had no idea. I wasn't expecting this.

It was true that I'd wondered why he never mentioned his father, but I always assumed there must've been an unpleasant divorce, or he'd died, and he simply didn't want to discuss it.

I leant forward. "How awful! You never met him? That's so sad. Do you want to talk about it, tell me what happened?"

I was mortified. How unsettling it must've been for him, never to have a father in his life – never to have him read a bedtime story, watch him in school plays, celebrate his successes – do all the things that fathers do.

He swallowed hard, gathering his strength. "He left mum when I was about six months old and once I was able to understand that he wasn't going to come back, she was adamant that I must never try to contact him."

My cheeks were burning. "*What*? Never? What about birthdays and Christmases? Didn't he try to get in touch with you at all?"

I could hardly believe what I was hearing. Not to get in touch with your own child? Surely no father would do that.

He frowned. "Sadly, no, he never did. I had no address for him, and the few times he wrote to me, Mum tore up the letters before I got a chance to read them. She never knew I saw her do it."

I caught hold of his chilled hand.

"So ... I had a fatherless childhood. No role model. The result is – I have no idea how to be a 'good father' and I don't want to risk making a total mess of it."

I stroked his hand. "Oh Steve," my eyes did their best to hide my tears, "it must have been dreadful for you. Sounds as if he wasn't a very loving person, never wanting to get to know his son."

I watched his face, wishing there was something I could say to make it better, but I didn't have the words.

I never met Steve's mum; he told me she died of cancer when he was a teenager, and he went to live with his grandparents. I wish I'd had the chance to speak to her, but no doubt she wouldn't have wanted to talk to me about it.

It might have helped Steve, though …

*

Selfishly, I hoped he would mellow in his view of fatherhood as time went on. After we got married, he pretended to be disappointed at our failure to conceive, but he couldn't hide his secret relief, and his life-long sadness at his own father's lack of love for his son.

I loved my dad to bits. When I was a child, his was the comforting hand I held when he took me to see the doctor or dentist; his was the gentle voice that told me bedtime tales and he was the lovely dad who pretended to be Father Christmas, dressed up in mum's red hooded dressing gown.

As I got older, he was the one who taught me to swim, how to look after my pet rabbit, and encouraged me to climb trees and make dens. And he had looked forward to the day when he'd 'walk me down the aisle'. Steve had never experienced any of those precious times.

I cannot begin to imagine how it must feel to only ever know *one* parent. There would always be something important missing, something *very* important …

*

I put my concerns about Steve to one side, and foolishly start collecting things for the baby.

"Not a good idea," my best friend Kate tries to warn me. "You never know … best not to tempt fate …"

But I ignore her.

I find myself wandering around baby shops, unable to resist the tiny baby-grows, the soulful, one-eyed well-loved teddy in the charity shop toy basket, and the white-painted cribs in John Lewis.

And then – two days after the first scan – I lose the baby.

Steve pretends to be upset about it. "I know it's sad, but

perhaps it's for the best," he says, imagining – futilely – that his words might bring me some comfort.

"*For the best*? How can you say that?" I glare at him. "There was a new person growing inside me, who we would *both* have nurtured and loved. Once our child was born, you would have loved it, I know you would. You'd have had the chance to find out for yourself what it's like *to be a good dad.*"

I can't look at him. "All you care about is your music and your precious consultancy. Working at our marriage, deciding to try for a baby, has always come last on your agenda – if it was ever *there*."

I purse my lips. Poor Steve. I know it wasn't his fault that his dad left them, but I wish he *actually* shared my sadness about the miscarriage, rather than simply *pretending* he did.

I know in my heart that I must accept the truth – Steve and I becoming parents is never going to happen.

*

A dense fog of grief descends. As the weeks go by, the house takes on an air of neglect, the bed stays unmade, and takeaways become our normal fare. And then the cleaning obsession arrives to control my days. But however hard I try, there is a space in my life, which I believe can never be filled.

All I long for is my child: to love, to nurture, to hold in my arms.

And in my heart.

I sink into a stagnant pool of desolation and deprivation. Once the obsessive cleaning is finished, I watch rubbish TV, snooze after lunch most days, and I grieve for the child I will never see: the motherhood role I will never play.

Until I'm diagnosed, I see depression as simply self-indulgent, only affecting other people – until it descends to dominate *my* life with its spitefulness, smothering me.

Most nights Steve routinely falls straight to sleep, oblivious to my endless, silent tears. How is that even possible if he still loves me, like he used to?

Answer?

That's the point …

He doesn't.

"Have a good day," he calls, every morning, after breakfast. *A good day*? *Really?* He thinks I'm going to have *a good day*? He rushes off to his oh-so-important work upstairs in his home office, or to catch a taxi or a plane, focusing on any problem but ours, escaping from the reality of his feelings.

And mine.

I'm bereft. I have no role. I'm lost in a forest of tangled brambles, where I can find no paths to follow.

It can't be any clearer: I've been in denial about my sadness for far too long. I need to sort myself out.

I vow never to cave in again, never to turn back into *her*. I *will* stop my negativity, persuade myself there *is* a pathway out of my depression – all I have to do is find it. I'll make an appointment to see my GP, persevere with his medication and begin the search for the light which I'm convinced is waiting at the end of my tunnel.

It's time to leave the woman I hate behind.

Chapter 3

The squire

Ellen
September 1880

We are fortunate indeed in our village to be blessed with a kind and generous squire. This is not always the case – I've heard many tales of the arrogance and pomposity that some of the neighbouring lords of the manor show to their tenants.

Ever since he'd taken over the reins at Longmead House and the estate, our squire has overseen his staff with great care and consideration. There is barely a cottage in the village not lived in by one of his workers and their family. Each married man on his payroll is allotted a home as part of his wages, and as such, Father and our family have lived, rent free, in this cottage set aside for the head gardener.

But now, everything will change.

Despite knowing full well what action the squire will have to take, we are still humbled when he finds the time to visit us, a month after the funeral, to explain things.

He is sombre faced when Mother answers the door. "I'm so sorry, Mrs Freeborn. I'm afraid I've come to bring the news you were hoping never to hear."

She wipes her hands on her apron. "It's very thoughtful of you to visit, Squire, we all know you're a busy man. But you're quite right, what you have to say won't come as a surprise, and no mistake. Do come in and take a seat."

She manages to produce a small smile. "Before we go any further, Squire, allow me to extend to you our heartfelt thanks from all the family, for your generosity in organising the collection to pay for Mr Freeborn's funeral.

It was comforting to see so many of his workmates in the procession to the church. We're grateful to everyone involved."

She swallows and clenches her cold hands.

He is quick to respond. "There's no need for thanks, my dear. Your husband deserved the respect of us all and it was the least we could do for him."

I battle with my tears – and lose.

He continues, "After your poor husband's death, I'm afraid the time has come for you to leave this cottage. I have, at long last, been able to find a new head gardener, and he needs to start work as soon as possible. He and his family will be moving into this house, I'm afraid."

He can't avoid seeing our crestfallen faces. Despite knowing this day would inevitably arrive, it is still a struggle to hold back our tears.

His voice shows concern. "Please try not to worry. I'll do all I can to find you another home in the village, at a low rent."

I wipe my eyes before replying, "You are most kind, Squire. Once my husband has found fresh employment, I'm sure we'll soon be back on our feet."

His face grows serious. He is well aware of the predicament so many farm workers are finding themselves in, not only my Joe.

"Is Mr Martin looking for fresh work hereabouts?"

"Well, Squire, he was to start with, so he can stay living with us, but now he's having to search all over the county, and so far, there's no good news." I try to hide my fears about Joe's situation, but everyone knows – times are tough in the farming world.

The squire hangs his head. "I wish I could help him, but I'm afraid I'm not in need of any more staff at present. But in the meantime, I will keep him in mind, in case I hear of something suitable hereabouts."

I can see he is doing the best he can for us, but the fact remains that Mother simply won't be able to afford to start paying rent, unless Joe finds a new job.

Father's wages as head gardener had been high, as it was a specialist role and rewarded accordingly. But however hard Mother and I work, taking in as much laundry from our village neighbours as we can cope with, trying to scrape enough money together, she can barely manage to keep us adequately fed, let alone start to pay any rent on top. Despite her valiant efforts, her purse will be empty before the end of each week.

I can't imagine how she's managed to eke out our meagre rations since Father's death. Am I the only one who notices the small bowl she's started to use for her scant portion, in readiness for the inevitable move? And how she unfailingly gives me, Joe and our boys the largest shares at mealtimes?

I am proud of Mother for managing to address the squire without breaking down again. She speaks bravely. "We do appreciate you coming to speak to us, Squire. I hope your new head gardener will find this house to his liking." She discreetly blows her nose.

He stands up to take his leave and shakes Mother by the hand. "The new man will have a lot to live up to, Mrs Freeborn. Your husband was a credit to you, and I was certainly very fortunate to have him work for me." He turns around to give a forlorn wave as the garden gate clicks shut behind him.

The day we'd been dreading has arrived. Kind though the squire might be, the fact remains that the rent – even a small amount – will now have to be found. Mother is still having trouble sleeping of late, what with her grief, and now, with the never-ending worry and uncertainty about what might lie ahead, distress will only increase for all of us.

Most nights she puts her head under her bed clothes and sobs.

And so do I.

*

August 1911

Do you know how it feels to be gripped with fears for your future?

To dread the storm clouds that could be gathering for you and your family?

And do these worries keep you awake at night?

If I dare to look back to those distant nights – burdened with misery, any chance of sleep threatened by nightmare visions – I tremble, and hug myself to ward off the cruel forebodings that still haunt my mind after more than thirty years.

Chapter 4

Turning point?

Susie
September 2018

It all begins with another tedious trip to Sainsbury's.

I'm not in the mood.

At all.

It's raining and all I want to do is stay indoors with Mittens and immerse myself in my latest charity shop book bargain. How quickly my bedside pile of crime fiction has grown lately.

I park and scurry across the puddle-filled car park under my umbrella to collect a trolley – that's when it starts.

I know. I know something isn't right.

As soon as I catch hold of the trolley's handle, I sense it. My head is all over the place. I've got that feeling, the one you get when you find yourself outside your comfort zone, with no idea how to deal with the situation.

I start putting things in the trolley, but as soon as I try to set off for a fresh aisle, the trolley speeds up. I glance around to check if anyone is watching; surely someone must've noticed me struggling to keep control as it propels me along? I try to slow the wretched thing down, but it's a waste of time – the trolley is in charge. My face is flaming yet my hands are damp.

I've never felt so scared.

Completely out of the blue – or so I think at the time – it steers me over to the newspaper stand, where it comes to an abrupt halt right in front of the display of *Hampshire Chronicle*s, which I hardly ever buy since it's not exactly a riveting read. I stand still for a bit, not sure what to do next, when something tells me I have no choice: I *must* buy a copy. I can't ignore it. Anything to appease the wretched trolley.

I grab the paper and hurriedly pay for it at the quick checkout before shoving it into one of the paid-for bags of groceries. I dash out into the car park, relieved to be in the fresh air again, able to say goodbye to the spooky trolley. I don't bother to take it back to the stand; I simply abandon it.

I dump the shopping in the boot as fast as I can, open the driver's door and flop down in the seat. Once the door clicks shut, I feel safe. I tell myself to calm down and I try to figure out what this is all about. I dry my hands on my jeans, and tidy my bedraggled hair in the car mirror, while the welcome warm air from the heater starts to chase away the dampness – but not my unsettled feelings.

I clutch my phone, with cold hands. I know what I have to do: I must ring Kate, my oldest friend, and confide in her, bring it all out in the open, to make it *real* – which of course it is.

*

"You sounded dreadful on the phone, Susie; whatever's the matter?"

Kate has arrived and our coffee is made. We settle down at the kitchen table.

I take a much-needed deep breath. "I *had* to see you – I want to tell you the whole story."

"*The whole story?*" She grins. "Okay, what've have you been up to now?" The chocolate digestives are going down well.

"Well …" I try not to giggle. "It all started with a mundane trip to the supermarket …"

She almost chokes on her coffee, "Of course it did!"

I go on, "Seriously, Kate, you couldn't make it up!"

She puts down her mug and gives me a supportive grin. "Come on – tell me what this is all about."

I smile at her. "It's important you take me seriously, though. Please don't laugh. It's all true. Trust me."

"Of course I won't laugh, but I want to know all the details, however silly you might think they are."

She sips her coffee and helps herself to another chocolate biscuit. I sit up straighter in my chair and take a moment. It's such a relief to talk to Kate, to get the whole episode out into the real world.

*

After finishing my story, I get up to make some more coffee, waiting for her reaction.

She leans back in her chair. "Well, I have to say, Susie. I'm lost for words, which – as you know – isn't like me! This is an extraordinary tale, that's for sure, even for you." She raises her eyes to the ceiling. "Mind you, you always have led an exciting life!"

I grin at her.

"But seriously, it doesn't make sense, does it? It's no wonder you were scared. Had you picked one of those wonky-wheeled trolleys? They do have a mind of their own."

"Yes, I know what you mean, but no, I checked, and the wheels were fine."

"So ... you bought it? The Hampshire Chronicle? I rarely do anymore."

"I did, and that was the key to it all. Wait till you here the rest!"

Kate bites her lip. "Are you still feeling unsettled, Susie? You're looking a bit flushed!" She giggles again. "Come on, I can't wait to hear episode two!"

Kate's eyes have hardly left my face throughout my story. She raises her eyebrows and passes me her mug and I pour us both a fresh coffee before picking up from where I left off.

"I'm sure you can imagine how relieved I was to be home, in my safe space. I unlocked the back door, flung my raincoat over a chair and heaved the shopping bags onto the worktop. I quickly put everything away, desperate to relax with a hot drink, to go over what had happened."

"You must've been more than a bit bewildered at all this," Kate adds.

I nod. "I certainly was. But I had no doubt – whichever way I looked at it – everything I'd experienced in the supermarket was *real*."

I take another deep breath, hoping against hope she'll take me seriously. "I decided that after the hiatus in the supermarket, I might as well give the wretched newspaper a quick flip through; there might be an ad for a teaching position."

Kate knows I've been looking for a new job.

"I explored the situations vacant columns, finding nothing that took my eye, only to be left with the rest of the paper, with its predictable articles about WI meetings and planning applications."

She smirks, knowing exactly what I mean.

"And – here comes the turning point …" I give her a wink and she leans forward to put an encouraging hand on my arm. "As I pushed the rest of the paper aside, the *Property For Sale* supplement slipped out of the centrefold and grabbed my attention."

Kate raises her eyebrows. "You didn't tell me you were thinking about moving to a new house?"

"No, I didn't – because we weren't! But I got the same feeling I'd had in the supermarket – scanning the property pages was something I *must* do. My hands shook a little as I spread the supplement out on the table to get a clearer view, and *there it was!*"

Kate bites her lip. "There was *what*, Susie?"

I beam at her. "A magical photo of a pretty cottage in Hursley. It caught my full attention, straight away."

I can see Kate is at a loss about what to say.

"In hindsight, I honestly feel that this explains what the bizarre scene in Sainsbury's was about. I was *meant* to buy the local paper and I was *meant* to see this particular cottage for sale!"

Kate nods. "I know you've often dreamt of living in a cottage, so I'm not a bit surprised you were excited."

Grins appear on both our faces.

I go on. "Despite my 'sensible head' telling me not to be so silly, I found the estate agent's web site on my phone. And there it was, the full description. I read it over and over, taking in every detail. It spoke to me – and I listened."

Kate stands up, taking her coffee – now cold – over to the sink to pour it away.

She turns towards me. "Do you mind if I have a look?"

"Of course. I've been dying to show you. I've printed the details off upstairs, ready for Steve when he gets back at the end of the week from the States."

I hand her my phone. "Here's the website, I can print you off the details if you like."

Her face is a picture. "And what are you going to do next?" As if she hasn't guessed.

I'm quick to reply. "Oh, you know what I'm like – there was no way I would risk losing my momentum – I had to follow it through."

She beams, knowing full well what I'm going to say …

"Yes! I did! I acted on impulse and made an appointment to view the cottage."

Now it's my turn to giggle. "Well … let's face it, if I wait for Steve to return from his trip it'll be too late, the cottage will be under offer. We all know that a reasonably priced property in a desirable village never stays on the market for long. And we also know that if he were here, he'd dismiss the idea without a second thought. He'd tell me I should be content with my lot, pull myself together and go back to teaching."

She sighs. "Well, this is a lot for me to take in. For a start, where on earth has all this come from? Why would you suddenly be looking at houses for sale in our local rag?"

I want to keep her onside. "I know, it does sound

strange, but I'm convinced there's something powerful, beyond my control, in the driving seat. This is much more than a sudden desire for change. It's a *compulsion* – impossible to ignore. Instinct, intuition and imagination have taken control."

Kate gives me a huge hug, and I feel so much better now I've confided in her.

As I watch her drive away, I sense my earlier scary feelings receding. Very slowly, at the far edges of my mind, a faint hope for a possible new start is emerging, like gentle candlelight tempting me to follow its flickering pathway out of the dark.

Chapter 5

My insides curdled

Ellen
September 1880

Uncontrollable tears tumble down my flushed cheeks as I lean back to relieve the pain in my knees, my hands red raw and throbbing from scrubbing our brick kitchen floor. I'm willing to tackle any relentless chore if it will keep my mind from drowning in formidable forebodings.

Finally, I give in, and utter these fateful words out loud in our empty kitchen. *"We have no other choice."*

Despite Mother and I slaving away at our laundry work, the dreadful truth has to be faced, there is no point in pretending otherwise. Despite the squire's kindness, we can't manage to pay the rent, with Father gone and Joe out of work.

The workhouse it will be for me and our boys.

The prospect haunts my dreams: distressing cruelty, near-starvation and never-ending toil – that's what I've heard we'll have to endure. The tales I've been told in the village refuse to leave my mind:

'Most inmates go on to live out their days in the "house". They only leave in their box for their pauper's funeral. You get stale scraps to eat and they force you to work until you drop.'

Everyone says the same.

And in return for what?

A roof over our heads, scant portions of food in our stomachs, relentless humiliation, and hardship for the rest of our days. Father would've wrung his hands in anguish if he'd had any idea of what would befall us after his death.

*

We're not the first in Bishopstoke village with no choice but to bow to fate and seek a place in the Hursley Union Workhouse, and sadly, we won't be the last. There are several families nearby who've been obliged to leave their beloved homes after misfortune turned them into pitiful paupers, brought low by the scourge of destitution.

But now it is *our* family who must confront the inescapable truth: any glimmer of hope of staying together has been firmly snuffed out. Nightmare images impossible to ignore fill my head, of the misery and misfortune that awaits us if we're given a place. I shudder every time I dare to imagine it.

Is it truly a *crime* to be a pauper? Is it fair to be viewed as failures in the eyes of our more fortunate peers? It's well known there are plenty of feckless scroungers and malingerers about, who do not deserve to receive indoor relief, however much they insist they do. All they achieve is to give us honest folk a bad name. We are neither scroungers nor malingerers – far from it. We've made every possible effort to manage. After all's said and done, no one *chooses* to be dependent on others for their living and to be shamed for their poverty; the house is but a last resort, to be avoided until every other avenue has been explored. And now it has.

Sadly, for our family, and for many before us, we have no choice.

At least, not as far as we know …

*

Our fate will lie with the board of guardians: a committee of wealthy landowners and businessmen appointed by local ratepayers to be responsible for organising indoor poor relief.

When the squire heard we weren't coping, he was shocked and saddened. He kindly helped us put our names forward to be considered for places, and a meeting with the board of guardians has been arranged.

Every unfortunate seeking indoor relief must face the ordeal of telling the guardians their sorry stories. Humiliating it might be, but the fact remains our future rests with them. It is up to us to show we are destitute, before they will even consider our application.

I pray they will see their way to being generous, though my insides curdle at the thought of what their decision will mean for my two boys and me, and for poor Mother, who has done everything she can to keep us at home with her.

With heavy hearts we tramp the four-mile journey to present our case, fear fuelling each reluctant step, forcing us forward, despite our longing to turn around and hurry back the way we've come.

Poor Henry's feet quickly become sore as he struggles to keep up, his toes poking out of his shabby, too-tight boots. Mother and I take turns to carry little James for most of the way, along field paths choked with brambles, over stiles, and through dense, dank woods. Henry does his best to help, giving his young brother rides on his back, despite the pain in his feet that is plain to see.

He tries to reassure us. "I'm the man in our family for now, Mother. Don't you fret; I'll see we're all right. Father will be proud of me, for taking his place."

I slip my arm around his young shoulders and my cheeks burn with pride and love. A mere twelve years of age, but with the heart of his father beating strongly inside.

At long last our wretched journey is nearing its end. Unsettling rivulets of anxiety run through my veins. We stubbornly refuse to look for long at the signpost looming at the fork in the road, choosing instead to gaze back along the path we've taken.

We dilly-dally … until it's impossible to put it off a moment more.

Chapter 6

Right in front of your nose

Susie
September 2018

The cottage refuses to let me go.

I'm captivated by everything I've seen online. I can't stop poring over the details, enthusing about the pictures.

And – oh my goodness – it has beams, and an open fire.

The more I think about it, the more I know there is no question that this is meant to be. If we'd ever thought about moving, this is exactly the area I would have investigated: the charismatic Hampshire village of Hursley, a few miles south of Winchester, with its unique brick chimneys and timber-fronted Tudor houses.

I grew up two miles away, in the catchment area for the village school, and I loved every minute of my years as a pupil, enjoying the freedom and fun of childhood. Hursley had played an important part in my past, when every day felt carefree, far too long ago.

I've heard it said that when you're searching for the answer to a problem, you'll often find it … right in front of your nose.

So, would a move to Hursley help me find the answer to mine?

*

All of which explains how I come to be sitting in my parked car, in the early evening, gazing out at an unlit lane in Hursley village, about to view the cottage, unable to stop grinning.

I use my torch as I approach the black metal gates that

lead into the Square, which in fact isn't a square at all, but a rectangular courtyard, partially enclosed by two and a half terraces of slate-roofed cottages. The agent told me they'd been restored not long ago, after lying derelict for many years. The one I'm about to view is in the middle of a row, its porch light beaming a warm welcome.

I stand still, alone in the quiet lane, with my eyes closed, savouring the unique smell of autumn wood fires in the damp night air. I could stay here, by myself, breathing it in forever.

A car draws up and Anna, the young attractive estate agent, gets out. She shakes my hand.

"Mrs Welch, lovely to see you. Mrs Howard is expecting us."

I follow her along the grey, brick-patterned path to the open front door, where Mrs Howard is waiting. I wonder if she'll notice the sparkle in my eyes.

Anna carries out her guided tour, full of enthusiasm for the décor and atmosphere, but I could have saved her the trouble; she has no need to 'sell it' to me. There's no question about it – it will be ours.

Here are the ancient black beams, the open fire in a brick fireplace, a nook for our grandfather clock, all contributing to an intriguing, irresistible pull to the past. I follow Anna to explore upstairs, which proves equally alluring with sloping ceilings, and low, wide window sills begging to be transformed into cushioned window-seats.

A definite air of seduction fills the cottage. No need to tell Mrs Howard I admire her home – she only needs to look at my face.

I used to think that people who trusted in notions like fate, astrology and destiny were a bit crazy; surely, we should take responsibility for our *own* decisions, our *own* choices and our *own* paths in life. I also thought I had a sensible head, full of old-fashioned common sense, the last person ever to be persuaded that there were *'influences'* beyond our understanding, beyond our control … that is until this evening, when I have that sensation when you know for certain that the choice you're about to make has already been made.

The cottage has chosen me.

Chapter 7

Moment of truth

Ellen
September 1880

We're almost there, bravely traipsing towards Hursley, making the distressing, degrading journey to meet the board of guardians – a petrifying prospect.

I screw up my eyes to peer at the words etched in the wooden signpost: *'Hursley 1 mile'*. I wrap my arms around my boys for a wee bit longer, before we must drag ourselves away from the crossroads, desperately longing for a reprieve, subdued by the grim fear that consumes us.

We struggle along the deeply rutted cart track, passing a few cottages on the outskirts of the village, eventually slowing to a dawdle, each of us trying to put on a brave face for the sake of the others.

But we can skirt around our fate no longer. We huddle together at the end of the loathsome lane where the workhouse waits, before cowering in front of its imposing, intimidating, rusting iron gates, studded with angry metal nails. I reach up to tug the fraying rope hanging from a large brass bell to announce our arrival, its ominous clang sending tremors through us all. We stare, aghast, as the gates grind open, dragged by two unfortunates.

Our stomachs are quickly assaulted by the sickening smell of cooked cabbage from somewhere inside. We cover our noses and mouths with our mufflers at the stench of what appears to be a cesspit overflowing into the lane, while flies buzz around the foetid water. I picture unseen inmates peering gloomily out at us, recalling the day of their own fateful interviews.

We're ushered into the building by a kindly looking

individual, who, astonishingly, turns out to be the master. I gaze around at our surroundings, preparing to be faced with a miserable, menacing institution.

I nudge Mother and manage a small smile as we're confronted with two neat terraces of slate-roofed cottages, not in any way like the imposing edifice I'd feared. I square my shoulders and take a soothing breath, but my anxiety stubbornly refuses to be chased away.

Mother's distress worsens when we're left to wait in a dim, gaslit corridor, outside what turns out to be the guardians' boardroom. She paces up and down, trying in vain to keep her anguish to herself. "There's no other choice, Ellen," her handkerchief is soon sopping, "not until your Joe comes home with news of regular work and a pocket full of money."

She is well aware – as am I – that the future of our family will be decided in a few agonizing minutes.

Mother is not the only one at the end of her tether by the time the weighty, studded oak door creaks open and the chief guardian summons us through. The bleakness of the boardroom only serves to underline the austerity we'll no doubt endure in the house – it's a stark, sombre room, made gloomier by walls panelled with dark wood, barely lit by two hissing gas lights, and grimy, cobwebby glass rattles in the ill-fitting windows. A depressing air of dampness and despair fights with an eye-watering cloud of cigar and pipe smoke that has stained the ceiling over the years.

The guardians lounge around a well-worn oak table, occasionally tugging at their stiff starched collars, peering at us through the smoky haze. It's the responsibility of these few affluent men to judge whether we are *'deserving poor'* – or not.

We wait, reluctant to move.

There they sit, haughtily doing their duty: nine ruddy-faced, portly gentlemen, stomachs bulging against tight-fitting waistcoats, side-whiskers bushy as fox's tails.

I look up to read the supposedly uplifting motto

displayed in a black painted frame on the wall, for every pauper to see: *'Blessed Are The Poor'*. How I wish that were true.

Mother is near to collapse when we are beckoned forward to stand in front of our judges. I gently squeeze her cold, trembling fingers, gathering my boys close with my other hand.

The chairman's voice is surprisingly gentle. He addresses Mother first. "Mrs Freeborn. You have come to us to plead for an offer of the house. I assume we are your last resort."

He comes across as a beaming, charitable-looking man of large girth, who shifts about uncomfortably in his bow-backed chair before he stands up to shake her hand.

"You are asking us to admit your daughter and her two children to this house." Hearing those ominous words sets Mother off again. It is not only the smoke in the room causing her eyes to water.

"As you know, we're here to assess your case. You must tell us how it has come to this. Why is your husband no longer able to provide a home and a living for his family?"

Mother clears her throat, stammering a little. "It's ... like this, sir. Things were going well for us – he was a hard worker, never one to take his money to the public house –" a sudden embarrassed coughing from one of the guardians interrupts her – "and we managed well enough. He had a well-paid job as head gardener on the Longmead estate in Bishopstoke and our cottage was allotted to him as part of his wages."

Her voice reflects her pride. "Well thought of by all the staff he was; you could ask him anything about plants. He was specially known for growing exotic fruits in the glasshouses, to impress the squire's dinner guests. He was an expert at growing pineapples, apricots and grapes for the table." A small smile flickers across her wan face, and the boys stand up straighter and grin at each other at the thought – how they would love the chance to taste such luxurious fruits.

The chief guardian continues. "And how did he come to lose his job? You've told us the squire was pleased with his work."

Mother's gaze drops to the floor. She clasps her cold hands together and I watch her struggle, her voice weakening almost to a whisper. "He ... got ill, sir. I couldn't afford the money for a doctor ... and he was ... taken from us, sir."

The chairman's face softens. Another embarrassed cough disturbs the weighty silence.

Mother struggles to compose herself before continuing. "The squire has kindly permitted us to stay in the cottage, rent free, for the time being, sir, but now he has informed us that a new head gardener has been found, and we'll have to move into a smaller home, and start paying rent. I can't afford to feed my daughter and her boys, as well as myself, let alone pay rent on top. You can imagine that the money my daughter and I earn from our work as laundresses doesn't go very far."

The guardians puff pretentiously on their cigars, blowing out pompous plumes towards the ceiling, their spectacles perched on the ends of their noses. They look the boys up and down.

The chairman continues to take the lead and turns to me. "Now," his look grows more serious, "Mrs Martin. Tell us about the situation regarding you and your children."

I stand as proud as I dare but feel shy of looking him in the face. My voice echoes around the cheerless surroundings. "Well sir, my Henry here, he's twelve years of age and little James is four."

"And ... you have a husband?"

Those pairs of judgemental eyes again.

I nod, fiddling with my wedding ring.

"And does he have a trade?"

"Oh yes, sir, my Joe is a hard-working farm labourer. Turns his hand to most things on the farm he does; we were distraught when he was laid off. But as you know, labouring jobs aren't easy to come by these days, what with the run of bad harvests and those steam-powered machines taking the place of many of the men. He's doing the rounds, far and wide, searching for work, sir. Once he gets taken on again, and earns a regular wage, things will improve, and we can return to live with Mother. You can be sure we won't prevail upon your generosity for very long."

The guardians share cynical glances. They think I won't notice.

I do.

"Well, Mrs Martin, if we decide to admit you and your boys, you will be kept busy and no mistake. The house-laundry will be fortunate to have a strong, healthy young laundress like you to work with them. You will also assist in the kitchen, carry out daily cleaning duties and help with the making and mending of clothes."

The back-breaking work I'd done with Mother of late, taking in endless piles of washing and mountains of mangling, would stand me in good stead by the sound of it.

They put on a show of discussing our fate, huddling together, muttering inaudibly, sending yet more clouds of expensive smoke into the room, making sure we are fully aware of their generosity, and duty-bound to be grateful if they grant us places.

They expect us to feel *grateful?*

I try to comfort Mother with a hug while we wait for their judgement, and James and Henry make themselves as tall and grown up looking as they can.

I turn my wedding ring again, around and around.

Our moment of truth has arrived.

The chairman squeezes himself out of his chair and stands in front of the table, hitching his thumbs behind his braces.

He addresses Mother. "Mrs Freeborn. I'm pleased to tell you we *are* disposed to grant your daughter and her two boys places in this house. They will be admitted a week from today after breakfast. Matron will explain the procedures to you after this meeting."

A week from today.

We'll be saying goodbye to our home in seven short days. At least – for now.

A few momentous minutes, that's all it took to seal our fate. My hands are shaking and I long to be anywhere but here.

Somehow, I manage to mutter, "You are most generous, sirs."

The boys search my face for any reassuring sign that everything will work out well. I produce the smallest hint of a smile for their sake, grasp their hands and pull them close again.

The guardians stand up to watch us leave, virtuous smiles on their florid faces, before we hear the cumbersome oak door close behind us.

We face our return journey in sorrowful, subdued silence. So many disturbing, unanswerable questions clutter up in my poor head while we traipse home.

How will my poor boys survive in such a place?

When will Joe return?

Will we have to stay in the workhouse indefinitely if he can't fulfil his promise?

This is the most shameful fate that could ever befall anyone.

I want to scream.

*

Ellen
August 1911

All these years later the workhouse remains a feared institution, despite the improvements I've heard about: gaslight has replaced candles and oil lamps, and I gather the food is much improved. Nevertheless, the fact remains: no one chooses *to be dependent on others for their living, and to be humiliated for their poverty.*

Chapter 8

Mesmerising ...

Susie
September 2018

We're in the kitchen, having a drink (or two) before supper; I'm hoping a couple of lagers will help chase away Steve's grumpiness. He's not long unpacked after his trip to the States and jet lag has aggravated his irritable mood.

Once he's drained his first glass and our food is on the go, I slide the estate agent's details across the table. "I'd like you to take a look at this, love. Don't worry, it's only an idea; I'm not committing us to anything, but I'd love to know what you think."

I wait while he skims them through before tossing them to one side. He leans back in his chair, his face clouded. "Okay, Susie. Tell me what on earth this is all about."

I keep my cool and wait.

He raises his voice. "What do you expect me to say? Are you seriously telling me you think we should *move house*?"

I square my shoulders, preparing for the discouraging words I'm about to hear, foolishly hoping they will stay unsaid.

He pours a second beer and heaves an all too familiar exasperated sigh, before continuing. "What is it with you at the moment?"

My heart lurches as malignant moths crowd together in my chest. I swallow down the words I wish I had the confidence to say.

He's on a roll. "For goodness' sake! I fly off for three weeks to important business meetings, leaving everything hunky-dory at home – or so I thought – only to come back to hear that *you've* decided we should move. And not to a *house*, to a tiny *cottage* in Hursley! What on earth were you thinking?"

I have to admit he has a point; after all, it must have come as a bit of surprise: as far as he was concerned, we hadn't been talking about moving, hadn't raised the subject.

Not until the cottage took charge.

But he shouldn't be surprised at my interest in this particular location; he knows I've always had a soft spot for Hursley and its cottages. He's heard me enthuse over their age and unique character many times when we've driven through on our way to Winchester, and I've often enthused about how much I loved my years as a pupil at the village school.

I stare, preoccupied, at my empty wine glass, rolling its stem back and forth in my fingers. I get up to fetch the bottle from the fridge, mainly to have something to distract me, to give me a moment.

Steve blunders on, "There's nothing wrong with this house – in fact it's perfect for us. Plenty of room for overnight guests, decent size garden, brick barbecue, double garage. What on earth's made you decide we ought to move?"

I try again to tell him – fearful of imminent tears – that it was only an idea, nothing more. It's not easy to explain when he's being this antagonistic and, let's face it, I wouldn't have to explain if we were in tune, the way we were before …

*

Fifteen years together, but not *together* in the same way anymore. We've both changed, but not for the better. We've grown apart, especially over the past six months.

He can't relate to the person I've become since losing the baby – the miserable woman who lost her way and succumbed to depression – the woman without a purpose.

If I pressed him, he would insist that he understands the dark place I've sunk to, but at the same time he manages to pretend to himself that I'm dealing with it perfectly well. He thinks I'm satisfied with the superficial: retail therapy, *doing lunch* with friends, having my nails *done*. Of course, those fill my time and smooth the surface of my life, but that is all they do.

I persuade my face to produce a smile. "I know this house move idea sounds a bit, well, out of the blue – but believe me – it was a surprise to me too! It wasn't something I'd been planning; it just came to me as I browsed through the paper and saw the photo of the cottage for sale."

He bunches his hands on the table, letting out another long sigh, and purses his lips, staring – unseeing – at his empty glass.

I use my best positive tone. "The thing is, if we *did* move to a new house, it might help me find ... fulfilment. To find, well, you know, something to help me deal with what we lost."

He slowly shakes his head, eyes closed, making no comment.

"I've been feeling so much better since I saw the doctor again; ready to start looking forward, rather than backwards. I think perhaps a house move could be the answer. A change of scene, a fresh project."

I hurry out of the room to find some tissues to stuff in my pocket, just in case.

Back in the kitchen Steve is standing up now, ready for me. "What are you talking about? You want to find *fulfilment?* Deal with what we lost? For goodness sake, you sound like a therapist talking. It really is time you came to terms with it all."

I can't predict what he'll say next; but I prepare for his signature sarcastic tone.

"Are you still taking the antidepressants?"

How dare he ask me that? I stare down at the floor, trying to hide my wet cheeks. "As a matter of fact, I am,

Steve. And why is that? Because I need them. Full stop."

He has more to say. "It's not unusual to lose a baby, you know it's not, especially as you get older."

I open my mouth to reply but there are no words. My wedding ring is loose on my finger.

And he still hasn't finished his harangue. "There're plenty of women out there who'd swap places with you in an instant. I know you would've liked to have a baby, but it simply wasn't to be. Of course it's *sad*, but it's time you moved on. I have; it's six months now. You must start living in the present, not in the past. It's made you ill."

A storm of emotion is gathering. I have to stand my ground. "It's different for you, you've got your work. It's not like that for me; I haven't felt well enough to apply for another job. Not yet, anyway."

I keep a tissue in my hand, willing my tears to wait. "You know how excited we both were." He rolls his eyes. "Yes, you were too, although you won't admit it. We had something precious and life changing to look forward to. A house move could be a fresh start – for both of us. It would certainly give me a much-needed impetus. Won't you even think about it? Please?"

He's not going to be convinced. Oh well, perhaps I must accept it was a crazy idea – perhaps I *have* got a bit over excited.

He fiddles with the details, reluctantly. "I've had a quick glance through these, and, for a start, the cottage is nowhere near big enough. Where on earth would we put everything? I wish you'd waited at least until I'd had time to look into it properly, before getting so caught up. I'm guessing you've given the agent the impression we're definitely going to put in an offer?"

He opens the fridge to fetch a third lager.

I wait – again – with my empty glass in my hand, but it goes unnoticed and I end up pouring my own. I take a restorative gulp. "Okay, you're right: I admit I did get a bit carried away, but how many times have we said how pretty Hursley is? And you know how much I love older properties –"

I stop, mid-sentence. The estate agents' details ... on the table ...

Mesmerising ...

Could it be the effect of the wine? My chest starts to pound, but not in a good way.

Why hasn't Steve noticed?

The details are fluttering – insistently – with no sudden draught to cause them to move.

Are they twitching to get his attention? Could they be trying to tempt him to agree to buy the cottage? Or am I imagining things ...

He remains oblivious, raising his voice. "Do you honestly expect me to go along with this crazy idea of yours? Yes, we might like the village but that doesn't mean I'm going to uproot from a perfectly adequate four-bedroomed house to move into a poky little cottage. Where am I going to have my office? What about my music? And all my books and files? You know how much space I need in the study. After all, our home is where I make our living."

I lower my head and ache to add, 'A*nd it's where you assume I've nothing important to do...*'

He puts on his stoic 'don't think you're going to change my mind' face and downs his lager. I'd fully expected to have a problem winning him over, but I'm not about to let this opportunity go without a tussle. I settle myself back at the kitchen table and catch hold of his hand. "No point in throwing a strop about this, Steve. Let's talk about it sensibly for a moment, try to think outside the box."

He won't look at me.

"Apart from anything else, living in a home and a village brimming with history would be a fantastic boost for your business. Most of your clients are from the States; when they come over for a meeting with you, they'll be beguiled by the ambiance as soon as they walk through the door. Much more satisfying to have a meeting in a beamed cottage than in a run-of-the-mill modern house."

He obviously hasn't considered it from this aspect. His mouth twitches.

The details lie still now, resting, leaving the enticing coloured photo facing upwards. He picks them up to have another look. "Well …" he tries to disguise any seeds of interest, "I suppose it *might* be helpful for the business; Americans are impressed with anything *old*."

"And have you thought about the investment potential?"

Bingo.

I'm rewarded with a thoughtful silence. Have I hooked him?

He glances up at me from his bowl of cashews, munching noisily. I choose not to comment.

Instead, I play my winning card. "If we move, but after a while we find the cottage isn't big enough for us and we decide to sell, we wouldn't lose any money, not on a cottage in Hursley – in fact we'd make a good profit. Moving house would prove to be a win-win."

He exhales loudly before grabbing another fistful of cashews.

"At least agree to come and view it with me. No pressure; I promise."

He stretches and yawns. "Let's talk about this again in the morning. I can't deal with it now while my stomach's rumbling. How much longer before we eat? The airline food doesn't get any better and that was hours ago."

I go over to check the oven and my eyes are twinkling as I dish up our meal. I turn my back to hide a broad grin, as I pile a ridiculous number of roast potatoes on to his plate.

Yes, the food tastes good.

But so does victory.

Chapter 9

The loathsome lane

Ellen
October 1880

It's Monday morning, six o'clock, one week after meeting the guardians. The cottage is dark, the sun has not yet risen.

My head aches from lying awake and worrying. Sleep has failed to come to my rescue. Are we really destined to end our days in the house?

I'm worried about the boys; taking them away from everything familiar and friendly to live behind dank, damp walls. They'll be open to infections, imprisoned in cheerless rooms with nothing but dull days ahead. All we have left to cling on to is the fragile hope that my Joe will be our salvation, when he returns to tell us about his new job and rescue us from our misery.

None of us can find an appetite for breakfast this morning, despite the energy we'll need for the four-mile journey back to Hursley. Mother has wrapped up some bread and precious bacon fat in greaseproof paper for the journey, but I doubt it will get eaten.

With each shamefaced step that leads us away from our home and everything we hold dear, my mind is filled with thoughts of Joe.

Is he anxious about how we are managing without him?
Has he found a new position?
I pray every single night for his swift return.

*

After much deliberate dawdling, we trail through the

village once again until we reach the loathsome lane where the workhouse awaits. We loiter on the corner for as long as we dare, glad of any excuse to delay what we fear is coming. The boys stop to watch two pretty girls, about Henry's age with blue ribbons in their hair, bowling their iron hoops along the lane in front of us. Anything to put off the moment when we must bid Mother goodbye.

"We know where you're goin', we know where you're goin'," they chorus, pointing and laughing. I try so hard to hold my head high, but there is no hiding from them the reason we are here. Doubtless they've tormented downcast paupers time and time again, as they trudge their reluctant way through the village.

We shuffle around the corner where I can't help but cower again at the sight of the chilling iron gates; they tower above us, staring down in disdain, showing no mercy. Mother hangs her head and pulls her bonnet close around her pale face. I risk one last glance behind us, where those two be-ribboned girls are leaning against the wall, their hoops held still now, sizing us up with pitying – no longer mocking – eyes.

In spite of the experiences on the day of our interview with the guardians, we are still taken aback by the smell of dampness, over-cooked cabbage and stagnant water. It mixes with the stench of the reeking overflowing cesspool that we take great care to step around outside the gates. The comforting aromas of Mother's cooking will soon be but a fond memory.

How James sobs when his grandmother bids him goodbye. He grabs hold of her skirt in a desperate attempt to delay her departure. I do my best to stay composed, Mother struggles to do the same.

"Won't be for too long, loves." She almost manages a smile. "You'll soon be back with me, where you belong, you'll see, once your father comes home with good news."

Despite making every effort, her face belies the bravery of her words.

Dear Henry stretches up as tall as he can, and puts his

arms around her for one final cuddle. She ruffles his hair. "Try to do as you're bid, you two rascals. Don't get up to no mischief and they'll treat you right. Make sure you say your prayers every night before you go to bed; you can be sure God will be listening."

She withers in front of our eyes, crouched beneath her shawl, as she braces herself to watch the grim gates grind open to swallow us up. Beads of cold sweat trickle down my back and legs, and all I want to do is grab hold of the boys and run through the village and back home – a fruitless, foolish fancy.

I reach up a shaky hand to ring the rusty bell and the gates duly respond. We turn around to wave to Mother for the last time, failing miserably to stem our tears. The next few hours will be crucial.

Two people with an air of quiet authority are waiting for us on the well-worn pathway. It isn't difficult to work out who they are: the individuals we'd long feared to meet – the workhouse Master and Matron. We trail behind them, with fear in our hearts.

My first impression of Matron is of a tired, thin, overburdened woman of middle years, with a pallid face; someone with scarcely a minute to herself. Her straight, no-nonsense grey hair is held back from her face with black hairpins and I'm reassured to see the coarse apron she wears over her black dress is as white as the sheep in the fields. Her reddened hands show clear evidence of heavy toil, her sleeves rolled up above her elbows, ready to tackle her next chore.

The Master is not in any respect how I'd expected a workhouse master to be. After hearing the alarming stories in the village about larger workhouses, I'd pictured him to be a cruel, harsh disciplinarian with never a smile; but this does not describe the man standing in front of us this morning.

He is tall and thin, with a kindly manner, and clearly competent. His suit and waistcoat are clean enough but have seen better days, giving him an approachable air. He comes over as a man of moral character, thoughtful and practical, but content to allow his wife to take the lead.

Unsurprisingly, she is first to speak. "Mrs Martin. This is my husband, Mr Redford. He's the master here, taking charge of the men and the older boys. He organises and oversees all the men's work and also sees to the finances. You will please address him as 'Master' at all times."

Mr Redford soon notices Henry's tears and pats him gently on the shoulder. "Try not to fret, my lad. You'll be living with the other boys over seven years of age, over there on the men's side. Never fear, I'll be keeping my beady eye on you." He gives Henry an amicable smile.

Henry tries to dry his face to look across the yard, where a row of slate-roofed cottages awaits.

"Your mother and young brother will live on the women's side, but they'll be allowed to visit you for a short while on Sunday afternoons. I'm sure you'll soon make lots of new friends once you settle in at the village board school."

Henry glances up at me, still watery-eyed, trying not to look daunted at the mention of school, and a new one at that. I know how much he'd been looking forward to the chance to spend more days out of school with Joe in the fields, like he usually does, scaring birds away from the crops, sorting bundles of hay and helping to feed our Nellie and the chickens. He has been a huge asset to Joe, helping him out at busy times.

Matron smooths her apron, in a hurry to get down to things. "Young James here, he'll be your responsibility, Mrs Martin. You'll share a cottage apartment with three little girls and their mother. You'll take care of your James as well as helping out with the other younger children."

He cuddles up to me, nuzzling his face into my skirt, struggling to fight his fears. He'll miss his older brother, no question about it. They are close friends, in spite of the age difference, but now he'll have to fend for himself. How will he get on, living with three girls?

Matron glares down at him, her tone of voice matching

her facial expression. "Mind you," she sniffs, "he'll need a proper bath and haircut first."

I was grateful Mother never saw poor James hurried away for his 'proper bath and haircut', and thankful she didn't see his shrunken, woebegone face, almost impossible for any loving mother or grandmother to bear.

Now it's my turn.

At least Matron lets me keep my hair; it has always been my pride and joy.

"You're lucky it's not too long, my girl." She lifts the soft curls to take a closer look. "Much longer and you'd have had it cut, no question about that. Mind you, make sure you keep up with your daily untangling and checking, to keep any lice and fleas at bay."

I instinctively put up my hand to cover my mouth. Lice and fleas? They wouldn't last for five minutes in Mother's home, if she had anything to do with it.

I follow Matron into a windowless stone-flagged room where a grey metal bath waits, with a few inches of tepid water. I take off the clothes I'd travelled in, and shudder, blushing, as I lower myself into the bath, with Matron supervising. The carbolic soap burns my skin, just like at home, and there's only a rough, worn towel to dry myself with, clearly shared with the other women. I shiver as I clamber out, my whole body trembling as it drips water onto the cold floor.

I put on the shabby looking but clean workhouse uniform: a long, grey woollen dress over a red flannel petticoat, with a well-worn but freshly laundered white smock over the top. There are much-darned stockings and stiff black boots for my feet. I instinctively put my hand to my nose – I can't help noticing a strong smell of mildew.

I hand over my own clothes and Matron inspects them fastidiously to check I'm not hiding any valuables. Mother and I are only too aware of the rule: we daren't own *any* money or we'll be turned away; only our destitution qualifies us for places.

She bundles our things up in brown paper, ties it with

string, ready to be stored in one of her office cupboards with all the other inmates' belongings.

She makes it plain she considers our clothes to be unwholesome. "Ready for washing, disinfecting and safe keeping. Can't be too careful about avoiding diseases and infections in the workhouse, my girl. Medicines and doctors cost money."

I don't need to be reminded that we'd been unable to afford a doctor for dear Father, to ease his last days.

I decide to take a risk, and ask her, "May I be allowed to keep my bag with me, please Matron?"

Her lips tighten.

I plead, "It holds a few personal things of no worth to anyone but me, Matron, and would serve to remind me of home. I made it myself."

I try to remain calm while she pauses to tidy a few invisible stray grey hairs behind her ears. "Hmmm ... I'm not sure what the Master will have to say about that. It's a bit irregular, and I'll have to inspect it first, young lady. You could have the Crown Jewels in there for all I know."

She tips the contents on to the rough deal table in the office. She picks up my now empty calico bag, and puts back three handkerchiefs I'd hemmed myself, my Bible, a pencil-stub, some scraps of paper and a half-spent tallow candle, but she takes firm charge of the few matches Mother had spared me.

"No extra matches, my girl. You'll get a match when it's time to light your nightly candle." She doesn't miss the glistening of my tears and after a few seconds she leans forward to cover my cold, damp hand with her warmer one. "Oh, go on then. You can keep your precious bag. So long as you get yer chores done, s'pose there's no harm."

I manage a nervous smile and clutch my bag to my chest. It might not mean much to anyone else, but it contains all I have to my name.

At least, for the time being ...

Chapter 10

The clock's ticking ...

Susie
October 2018

I've been awake since the early hours, tossing and turning, my mind buzzing. Eventually I give up on getting any more sleep, leave Steve snoring, and go down to the kitchen to make an instant coffee and take a few minutes to gather my thoughts.

I'm remembering when he finally agreed to at least *view* the cottage, after he'd blustered and protested, trying not to give in ...

"Are you really sure about this, Susie? *Really, really* sure?"

It was the morning after I'd shown him the details and I'd made his favourite scrambled egg and smoked salmon for breakfast – not as a bribe, you understand, just as a 'treat'.

"Yes, I'm more than sure: I absolutely love the cottage."

He looked less than enthusiastic, but I knew I'd enticed him with my mention of an *'investment'*.

I cleared away his plate. "So, are you still going to come with me to view it today?"

Despite feigning a lack of interest, he nodded.

I didn't waste any time. "I'll ring Anna now to make an appointment. You never know, you might be entranced by it too!"

He put down the pepper mill, deliberating. "Well ... I suppose there's no harm in *looking*; let's get it over and done with and then we can get back to normal. There's a whole load of work waiting for me in the den." He grimaced.

I finished loading the dishwasher and said, "I'll do it straight away; no time like the present!"

And so it is that Steve and I have viewed the cottage ... together.

I'm not unduly surprised at his reaction, as we walk back across the Square to the gate and Anna asks him what he thinks of it, but I'm disappointed at his tone.

"Well, I suppose I can see why the cottage appeals to my wife, but – quite frankly – it doesn't do much for me."

Anna and I exchange knowing glances – after our earlier conversation on the phone, she knows exactly what she needs to say. "Your wife tells me you have an excellent business brain, Mr Welch; perhaps you could consider this purchase simply as a wise investment, too good to let it pass you by?"

She's found his weak point in one hit.

On the drive home Steve says no more about the viewing and I don't press him. Back in the kitchen I put the kettle on – and wait. They say, 'patience is a virtue'. For once I've found mine and it has its due reward: he actually smiles – yes, with enthusiasm – and announces, "Okay, let's do it. After all, what's to lose? I'll give Anna a ring and tell her we'd like to put in an offer."

I get up to put my arms around him before he heads off up the stairs, but he turns away.

"Need to get back to the office. I think we've had quite enough excitement for one day, don't you?"

I hear the office door close behind him.

Yes, perhaps it *is* enough excitement. *For now.*

*

The removal men will be here before too long.

Let's face it: I won't be shedding any tears at leaving. This house has never been a proper home; a cosy nest where children thrive, a place filled with squeals, squabbles and scraped knees from climbing trees and falling off bikes in the garden.

The time has come to pass it on, to a *proper* family.

I wrap my hands around my second mug of coffee and wander through the rooms for the last time, each one with labelled packing cases lined up, waiting.

Empty rooms – but not just empty of things. Yes, we'd made friends in our time here, and I don't know what I would have done without them, but friends aren't the same as family, are they?

I'm under no illusions. Steve is going along with this move purely as a way to impress his clients, to keep me out of his hair, and most importantly, to make some money if we ever move again; but at least he finally agreed. I catch myself wondering if it had helped that Anna was stunningly attractive and obviously fancied him ...

I get dressed, ready to watch out for the removal van from the sitting room window. Steve starts to carry his boxes of office paperwork out to the car until, finally, we wait *together* – for a change.

*

Gentle butterflies quiver in my chest as we make the short drive to Hursley. I perch on the high passenger seat in the removal van, while Steve follows in the loaded-up car. I want to hug the driver as we turn into the now familiar lane and pull up in the lay-by beside the black wrought iron gates that lead to the Square.

I stay put for a moment, taking time to gaze across the paved path to the cottage. I want to pinch myself – I still can't believe it's ours. The driver helps me down from my seat while Steve parks the car, piled up with his precious boxes of files. He strides ahead to open the gate into the courtyard, where a curious smell of cooked cabbage and dampness lingers in the air.

Out of time.

I hesitate for a few seconds, trying to take it all in, before I follow him through the gate and across the garden. Despite the autumn sunshine I sense a frisson, but not in a scary way. I feel an unseen presence, an enigmatic movement on the path, and the long grass by the kitchen door sways for a moment, as if someone has just brushed past. I glance around in case any of our new neighbours are about and I can say hello, but the courtyard is empty.

Steve takes charge of the keys and I wait on the front doorstep while he sorts them out. I smile wistfully to myself, remembering the day we moved into our first rented home together, a few months before our wedding. He gathered me up in his arms and 'carried me over the threshold', with a proud grin filling his face – back when we were young, naïve romantics living in a fantasy world, where married life would be like a fairy-tale.

But that was fifteen years ago.

Sadly, as we get older, we discover it rarely works out that way. Life has other plans, and some of us adapt to those plans better than others. Once we've made this move, I'm determined to find a future filled with optimism, leaving my past where it belongs.

Steve unlocks the front door without ceremony and carts in the first of the many plastic boxes he wouldn't have dreamt of entrusting to the care of the removal men.

It doesn't take long for them to sort the packing cases into their allotted rooms. They work tirelessly, sustained by multiple mugs of tea and chocolate biscuits. Once we've waved them off I allow myself to relax, to lie on the sofa and gaze up at the beams, indulging myself.

I have loads to keep me busy over the next few days and weeks – as Steve will be quick to point out, wasn't this the new start I'd craved? – and I'm looking forward to it, choosing where everything should go, transforming this cottage into our new home.

"Let's be lazy and have fish and chips tonight," I suggest, at six o'clock. I'm shattered now and could eat anything put in front of me. While Steve drives off to fetch our food, I make myself comfortable in front of the fireplace, listening to the soon-to-be familiar sounds of the cottage. The grandfather clock looks very much at home settled in its special nook, and will soon be ticking away once Steve has wound it up.

As I stare around the room, I can't shake off the feeling that there is something shadowy close at hand, wanting to make itself known.

Before we tuck into our meal, I notice it's beginning to feel unexpectedly chilly. I ask, "Shall we light the fire? I've brought some firelighters in case it's a struggle to get it going. Mrs Howard has kindly left us plenty of dry logs."

Steve glances over at the full log basket. "If you like, but be prepared for some of the smoke to blow back down the chimney. Often happens with old places, after summer's over."

Why does he have to spoil it? This will be our first open fire: well worth celebrating.

And oh, my word, it doesn't disappoint. The evocative smell of wood smoke: bare branches, brittle leaves, and bonfires – if I could, I'd bottle it.

We enjoy watching the flames while we munch our fish and chips out of the paper, licking greasy fingers as we go. The fire is proudly doing its job, with no smoke coming back into the room, and looking perfectly at home, when I hear it.

What on earth's going on?

It's the grandfather clock.

But it can't be. Steve hadn't set it going yet. So how come I can hear an ominous, slow ticking?

"What's that? Steve? Can you hear it? The clock's ticking! And it's so loud! Did you wind it up?"

"No, not yet. I told you, I'll have to arrange for someone to come and look at it. Those removal men should have taken more care. I don't know what you think you've heard, but I certainly can't hear any ticking."

I look over at our clock.

There is no mistake.

It. Is. Ticking.

And then ... I can definitely hear ... *footsteps* ... upstairs.

"Steve! Listen! Sounds like the bedroom floor's creaking, as if someone's walking about up there."

"Don't be silly, Susie. It's only the heat from the fire making the wooden floors expand. It's the first one of autumn, and the cottage is warming up."

I stare up at the ceiling, transfixed, suddenly conscious of the hairs on my arms. I shiver, despite the fire's best efforts, trying to persuade myself this isn't unusual – surely we must expect to hear lots of unexpected sounds in a cottage as old as this.

On a whim, I screw up our empty wrappings, put them carefully on the fire, with the new spark guard in place, and grab my cosy coat. I want to watch the smoke drifting skywards from the chimney. Steve makes a face, clearly thinking I've lost the plot, as it's getting nippy out there, but for me at least our first fire is something very special.

In the garden the trees are shrouded in smoke in the evening gloom. Tired now from the exertions of the day but buoyed up with adrenaline-fuelled excitement, I stand in the middle of our tiny lawn, wrapped in my warm red duffle coat, and gaze up at the misty sky, as the smoke wafts out of the chimney and away into the autumn air.

As I relish the sight and the smell, the garden darkens even more, until it's virtually pitch black and I can feel light rain in the air. A bit odd. I peer across the lawn into the darkness, convinced someone must have turned off all the lights in the village, or perhaps that there's been a power cut. I scan our new neighbours' cottages to check if they are dark too.

I'm getting cold. The only light to be seen is from a solitary candle guttering at a bare window, in the cottage opposite.

A *candle?*

This is more than strange …

A distinct smell of mildew and stale food surrounds me – like it did when we first arrived – competing with the wood smoke and the drenching drizzle that's ruining my hair and making me shiver under my coat.

It's time to seek refuge back in the warmth of the cottage. I shake out my rain-spattered coat on the doorstep before hurrying indoors, but when I check what's happening outside, through the kitchen window a few minutes later, all signs of rain have vanished. I wait a little longer, fascinated to see the magical porch lamp doing its job once more as it should, and a clear moon in a now cloudless sky lights up the garden.

Back in the comfort and normality of the sitting room, I stand with my back to the fire to warm up again.

Something makes me glance over at our clock.

Silence.

Was I mistaken about the earlier ticking?

I'll make sure Steve phones the repairer tomorrow; I want to hear it ticking *quietly* again, as it should.

We've let our cat out of her basket to have a sniff about in her new home, and she's been busy prowling around the edges of the room, as cats do in a strange place. But now she's stopped exploring and is crouching down at the foot of the stairs that lead directly out of the sitting room, ears pricked, green eyes wide, staring upwards.

"What's the matter, Mittens?" I whisper to her. "What's up?"

She sits perfectly still, gazing up the stairs.

At nothing.

She can see it. But I can't.

She stays there for what feels like several minutes but in reality can have been but a few seconds, her whole tail flicking and darting. I perch down next to her on the bottom stair, keen to follow her gaze and see what she sees, but it's not to be. There's nothing there. I must let my overexcited imaginings drift away, out of reach, along with the wood smoke.

My earlier sighting of a guttering candle at a bare window is pushed to the back of my mind.

And is that easy to do?

Strangely enough, it is – to begin with – to dismiss the sudden darkness in a rain-soaked garden, the creaks, the solitary candle, the ominous ticking, but I'm not about to tell Steve what I've experienced.

At least ... not yet ...

Chapter 11

Regular, plain but toothsome

Ellen
October 1880

'Taking the house'. An ominous option to be avoided if remotely possible – one that bad dreams are made of. I could never have envisaged that taking the house would lead me to believe in the unbelievable. It was surely a grievous fate that could only befall other people.

Or so we'd chosen to believe.

But – strange to tell – life in the house is not turning out to be as I'd feared. Yes, there are days when time appears to have slowed down, when I wonder if nightfall will ever arrive; and yes, it's dreary, the same routine day after day, no home comforts, nothing to look forward to, never enough to eat, a life filled with drudgery, constantly cleaning away dirt and dust …

Yes, it's harsh. Unrelenting. And however many times I tell myself our life in the house won't last forever, I know I'm not being completely honest.

But despite the exhaustion from all our hard work, we try to take care of one another as much as we can, keeping an eye out for our less mobile inmates, making sure the children are kept amused, trying our best to lift one another's spirits.

After my unspoken fears of how the Master and Matron would treat us, I am heartened to discover that few of my preconceived ideas about them have proved to be true; this workhouse is by no means a scary place to be. In fact – and I know this will sound strange – it turns out we are *fortunate* to be under their charge. We'd expected to be treated with disdain by staff who didn't care a button. Not so. Both of them are blessed with a kindly disposition and a benevolence I would never have thought could exist in those in charge of a workhouse.

Everyone can see that Matron is especially taken with the younger children, although she would never admit it. Some of the little ones are able to put away their shyness and will sit on her lap for a short cuddle when she spares the time, and occasionally she will read to them at bedtime, when she's finished her duties. It's reassuring to see how she's made their tiny playroom as comfortable as she can, with some well-used toys and picture books, kindly given by the ladies from the Hursley estate.

After talking to our fellow inmates, we learn that the guardians are so delighted with our Master and Matron – the conscientious way they carry out their roles, the care they give to all – they have presented them with a rare gift, in recognition of their long and devoted service: a fine grandfather clock, made by a revered clock maker, a relative of one of the guardians. It has been given a prominent place by the window, in the otherwise bleak office, where, every day, its ticking and chimes fill their hearts with well-deserved pride.

*

It's now three long weeks since we were admitted. I can hardly credit it. Three weeks of homesick days and nights and many tearful cuddles with my young James. But I cry tears of joy when Matron takes me aside one afternoon after I've helped clear our dinner away and washed the dishes.

She has exciting news. "Ellen – I'm pleased to tell you your mother has arrived for her first visit. She's waiting in the office."

I frantically wipe away my tears before crossing the yard, but I'm dismayed to see how exhausted Mother looks, her dear face pale, looking even paler against her black mourning dress and bonnet. She has trudged the four-mile journey alone, in the chill autumn weather; but she makes little of it, producing a soulful smile, despite her fatigue that's plain to see.

We've been warned that all visits will be supervised by Matron in this austere, dingy room, bare of curtains, housing a shabby table piled high with bulging dishevelled files, ink-stained ledgers and dog-eared documents and – in pride of place – the much-admired grandfather clock, to oversee proceedings.

After a reassuring hug, Mother is hungry for all the details about how we are faring. She is particularly intrigued to hear how few inmates there are. This little workhouse is proving to be one of a kind – in more ways than we could know.

I start to explain, "There are only thirty-five of us here, Mother, including ten children, in twelve little cottage apartments, each with two rooms. Men and women have their own 'sides'; the Master takes charge of the men's side and Matron oversees the care of the women and younger children."

Mother peers anxiously out of the window towards the far edge of the yard.

"And are you sure that Henry's coping over there, away from you and little James?"

I sigh. "You know how worried I was about both the boys, Mother. Joe had come to rely on Henry for extra help in the fields; he loved having a good excuse to take days off from school with his friends, to help with the harvest, and you know how much James enjoyed helping with our Nellie, always making sure she had enough food. She'll be missing him as much as he'll miss her." Our poor pig. We treat her like one of the family, but now she only has Mother to take care of her.

"But I needn't have worried; Henry has settled in far more easily than I could ever have hoped. In fact, he's the oldest of the boys, and he tells me the others already hold him in high regard. He's become a true leader of the pack."

Mother's shoulders are starting to lose their tension. She smiles a rueful smile. "He's taking on the role his father has left vacant. He's in charge! Joe will be so proud."

I don't mention my constant fear – that the boys' father might never return with good news – and I know Mother understands that Joe being taken on again is by no means guaranteed.

She has more questions. "And what about the older men? Do they fare well?"

I smile. "Most of them are retired farm labourers and, sadly, a few are feeble-minded, poor souls. Never been capable of making themselves a home outside, but they remain remarkably cheerful, and thankful to find a passable lodging in the house – a safe place to end their days."

"And what about you, love? How are you coping?"

I turn away, to hide my wet cheeks.

"I miss you Mother …" I give in, despite trying hard not to, and let my tears tumble. The forlorn expression on her face touches my heart. We share a lingering hug, unable to mask our mutual sadness.

Eventually Mother brushes away her tears and manages to produce a wan smile. "Tell me about the fare, love. Are the meals as we were warned they'd be? I suspect you're looking a little thinner, or is it my fancy?"

I'd tried, but obviously failed, to disguise my already diminishing size by putting on extra garments under my smock, not wishing to add to her distress. "The fare? Well …" I sense Matron's sharp eyes on me. "Our fare is regular, plain, but … toothsome. It falls to me to help with the work in the kitchen, preparing broth and peeling vegetables. We're …" I search for the words, "truly thankful for what we receive."

Mother's face shows her relief, but I can see she's under no illusions about our inevitably scant portions and not in the least deceived by my words of praise.

I continue, "We women eat our meals in our small day

room with the young children, and the men and older boys eat in theirs. We get excited on Wednesdays when – more often than not – we make suet puddings for dinner time. They fill us up, ready for our afternoon's work."

Mother and I exchange pertinent glances: her savoury suet puddings are legendary –Father's and Joe's favourite.

She asks, "And what about your living arrangements?"

We stand side by side to peer through the grubby office window into the barren, rainy yard beyond. Mother views the rows of cottages either side of the yard with undisguised curiosity.

I explain, "James and I share a single cottage apartment with Jane and her three girls. You can see how the house is arranged in two long rows, with the privies, the washing lines and the brick wall dividing us. Our apartment is the second door in the women's row."

While I'm pointing it out to her, I have to screw up my eyes, to make sure they aren't deceiving me. There's a distinct movement amongst the long grass by our doorstep; a movement not new to me but one – up till now – I'd convinced myself I'd been imagining. But this time there's no doubt. There it is, in the hazy light. I squint intently through the glass, catching my breath, saying nothing to alert Matron's attention. This would not go down well with her.

Mother's face softens as she takes everything in. "You're fortunate indeed to be so well provided for, love; all very different from our ..." she searches for the right word, "expectations."

Matron sends a grateful glance in her direction.

Mother has more questions. "Tell me about Jane and her family. How did they come to take the house?"

We step back from the window, and I try to tell myself I was wrong about what I'd seen amongst the grass. I answer Mother's question, trying to push the image away. "I feel blessed to live with Jane. I'm very fortunate – it's like sharing with a sister! She's a bit younger than me, with three daughters under seven years of age here in the house with her. James soon overcame his initial shyness about sharing with her girls. He's like a big brother to them. He likes to feel he keeps them in order."

"No husband?"

I stare down at the floor, twisting my wedding ring. "It's the old, old story I'm afraid – deserted her for another woman and left her with three children to bring up alone. He is a brickmaker by trade and brought in a fair wage, over in Brickfield Lane, for the new railway works in Eastleigh. But when he upped and left her, she was destitute. And she's under no illusions; she knows she'll never be able to find the means to leave the house."

Mother chews hard on her bottom lip while Matron discreetly moves away to busy herself tidying a pile of papers on her table that clearly need no tidying. I hear her sniffling.

We continue looking over the yard. "Our little cottage apartment over there is modestly appointed; we have two rooms, one up and one down. We share the bedroom with the children, sleeping top-to-toe, as we did at home with you, and with a flock filled mattress and a single blanket each we manage to keep one another warm enough. Yes, it's crowded, but cosy nonetheless. And this will make you laugh, Mother, James has been bravely helping Jane's girls to empty our chamber pots in the mornings, after a little 'gentle' persuasion!"

Mother can't help grinning at this telling revelation.

She continues, "And are you keeping yourselves warm in the parlour?"

"Oh yes, quite warm enough. We're allowed to light a small wood fire at sunset, once we see our breath making mist in the air. We have a corner cupboard with two cups and saucers, a Bible, a few books kindly given to Matron by the vicar's wife, and some well-thumbed newspapers. There are two wooden armchairs, a long wooden bench against the wall, and a potato-sack rug in front of the fire."

"You are blessed indeed." Mother's shoulders relax. "It cheers me to hear you have been given such a fair lodging.

And are you well provided with candles?" Her keen eyes have spotted Matron's candle-lantern on the table.

"Oh yes, we have sufficient. As darkness comes, we light one, although Matron sometimes 'mistakenly' gives us two if she sees a pile of mending or patching waiting to be done, and the firelight helps us see to do our sewing – we women do all the making and mending of clothes in the house."

Matron darts a glance at Mother to see how she receives this information and is rewarded with a grateful smile.

"And when are you permitted to visit your Henry, on the men's side?" Her face takes on an anxious frown.

I look down at my lap, my voice trembling. "I call out to him most afternoons across the wall dividing us when he goes out to play in their yard with the other boys after school, and James and I are allowed to visit him for a short while on Sunday afternoons."

I gaze out through the murky window while Mother sits down again to rest her walk-weary legs, in readiness for her return journey.

I remain where I am for a few moments longer, deep in thought, utterly unprepared for what happens next.

Chapter 12

Voices

Susie
October 2018

"When's the housewarming, Susie?"

"Can't wait to have a nose around!"

"Lucky old you – a country cottage!"

Our friends have been asking about a housewarming and I'm thrilled to bits to oblige. A party is exactly what we need. I can't wait to invite everyone to see our new home and I choose a date for later in the month, before Steve has to go away again, and to give us a chance to get straight.

I know many of our friends secretly think we're a bit crazy to move to a much smaller property, no doubt wondering how we'll manage to fit everything in. "Only two-and-a-bit bedrooms? It'll be like living in a dolls' house!"

It's true, it *is* tiny: two bedrooms in the main cottage and another in a separate annex across the garden, which Steve has been quick to claim as his den and office.

It suits him perfectly – it's detached.

Our last house was a new build, but it was far too big for the two of us, and after the miscarriage it took on a sterile atmosphere.

No charisma. But the cottage has charisma in spades. Buckets in fact.

It speaks to me. And I listen – to every word.

Steve is, not unexpectedly, reluctant about a party. "Better start making a list, but don't forget, we haven't got room for a crowd. We'll be squashed in like sardines if you invite too many."

I soon make the list and start to phone people. It already feels like we've been living in the village for ages. But it's only a couple of weeks, and here we are planning a party.

*

I'm ready.

I'm wearing my new long, blue velvety dress, specially bought for the occasion out of my clothes allowance.

"It flatters your figure," the trendy shop assistant had gushed. I doubt Steve will notice.

I blush as I check my appearance in the oval mirror on our bedroom wall, more than pleased to see the transformed woman who looks back at me these days. Not too bad for forty, I say to myself. I've inherited mum's youthful skin – few crows' feet yet and hardly a grey hair – and I've actually grown quite fond of my unruly auburn curls, which I'd hated as a child.

Before our guests start to arrive there's plenty of time to grab my duffle coat, throw it over my dress and pop over to the annex to fetch the flowers I'd bought in the market this morning. I'd put them in a bucket of water to keep fresh: multi-coloured hothouse roses, red, yellow, pink, and orange in bud. I've decided the cottage deserves flowers every week if I can manage it – fresh flowers for a fresh start – despite Steve's grumbles, insisting they are an appalling waste of money, as *'they only die'*.

Kate and her husband Graham are early. The moment Kate bustles through the front door, catches sight of the black beams and smells the wood smoke, she is full of enthusiasm, practically jumping up and down.

"Oh Susie! This cottage must have been built with you in mind. You were destined to have it!"

"It fits you like it was made for you. You love anything vintage, and now you've found the perfect vintage home. The grandfather clock sits snugly in that nook – I'm sure Steve will be getting it going soon. I know he takes a pride in looking after it."

I decide not to tell her that – no – he hadn't got around to it yet.

She's smiling, "And those roses ... perfect ... They add the finishing touch."

Neither do I mention anything about the loud ticking I thought I'd heard on moving day – there was no need. I'd obviously been mistaken; it was simply the excitement of the move getting to me.

But I admit I am surprised Steve hasn't wound the clock ready for the party.

Not like him at all ...

*

It's especially comforting having Kate and Graham to look round the cottage. She and I have been friends since teacher training college and have kept in touch ever since. I was delighted when she married Graham and took on a teaching post in Winchester. We spend a lot of time together. Graham has the knack of handling Steve, with his moods, and Steve's computer skills come in useful when Graham needs a hand, not being much of a 'techie'. They understand us, and we understand them, as only the best of friends can.

Kate and I conspiratorially sip our first glasses of wine in the kitchen, before the others arrive.

Kate whispers, "Dare I ask – is Steve a bit more positive now, about the move?"

"No, not really," I whisper back, leaning against the closed door to the sitting room, in case he can overhear us.

She rolls her eyes.

"He says men don't get excited about moving to a new house like women do. He still reckons we were mad to leave a four bedroomed detached house for a tiny terraced cottage, but once the estate agent pointed out its investment value, and I mentioned its appeal for his visiting American clients, he went along with it. You know what he's like, if there's money to be made …"

"Hmmm," she frowns, "you know what we think."

"Yes, I do, but you mustn't worry about me. At last I'm hoping to find what I've been looking for, since …"

Kate's encircling arms feel warm and safe.

She whispers again, "You know where we are, if ever – well, you know. If ever you decide …"

"Yes, I know, and I'm thankful for everything you both do for me." I clutch her hand. "He'll never admit it, but I can tell he's actually trying to make the best of it. He's set up the annex as his home office and den – somewhere to work, play his guitar, listen to music with Graham, and possibly get some peace and quiet."

"Peace and quiet? With his taste in music? You wish!" Kate banters, as I move away from the door to let Steve in to fetch a tray of glasses.

*

It doesn't take long for the sitting room to fill up with old friends and new neighbours. The fire behaves itself, looking like a Christmas card fire, showing off in front of our visitors. I can't remember the last time my face ached so much from smiling.

When all that's left of the food is crumbs and crumpled napkins, we gather round the fire to chat. It's Graham, with his wisdom, who starts us thinking, and before long there's a buzzy conversation going on about the history of the cottage, as we become more and more mellow with mulled wine.

"There's definitely a unique atmosphere here," Graham begins. "It feels like you're going back in time as you approach the Square. Mind you, talking of atmosphere, I could've sworn I smelled cabbage cooking as we came through the gate. For a moment there, I thought Susie might be dishing up those infamous Canadian cabbage-rolls of hers, as a special housewarming treat!"

I giggle. "Errr … No! Not after last time!"

What a disaster that had turned out to be. Graham and Kate had come to us for dinner at the other house and I'd experimented with a new recipe. However much they tried to be polite about them, the wretched cabbage-rolls ended up where they deserved to be – in the bin. The Indian takeaway came into its own that night. We laugh at the memory.

"Any idea how old this place is, Susie?" Graham is keen to start investigating.

I lean forward. "Well ... the agent told us this whole courtyard is Victorian. The buildings had been derelict for ages until a firm of builders converted them a few years ago."

Graham's face lights up. "You ought to try to find out a bit more; could have loads of fascinating history. It'd be intriguing to research who lived here, back in the day."

This has me hooked. He's right – it could be *very* intriguing.

Graham has planted a seed, and I'm picturing a bare candle-lit window…

*

Our last guest has left, and Steve has checked the fire is on its way out, put the spark guard in place, clearly getting ready to go up to bed, when there it is again: the slow, ominous tick of our clock.

But it can't be.

It's not possible.

Steve had told me he hadn't been able to get it working yet. He was going to find a local clock repairer to come and set it up. He thinks it might've been damaged in the move.

Mittens' ears are pricked. She stares up at the clock face, the tip of her tail trembling, before padding over to sit in the alcove by the fireplace, eyes fixed on the ceiling.

It's strange, isn't it, how animals 'know'? They have a unique ability to see and hear much that's hidden from us mere humans. If only they could tell us about it. Mittens 'knows'– and she's trying to share it – but I'm not ready to follow her lead. At least, not until she becomes impossible to ignore.

And then I hear what she's hearing. *Voices.* As if women and children are muttering, *upstairs*. As I stand near her in the corner, I notice how gloomy the room has become in the last few minutes and an unwelcome chill has taken hold. Has Steve switched off a light? Have we left a window open upstairs, causing a cold draught?

The clock is still making itself heard – loud and slow.

Steve glances over at me, one hand on the bannister. "I'm going up now, love, our warm bed calls. Got a load of paperwork to do tomorrow. Will you be much longer?" I don't reply, just shake my head, tap my ear and point up at the ceiling ... and over at the clock.

I give myself a swift talking to in my head, telling myself it must be our neighbour Joan's radio on the other side of the wall that I can hear. She'd warned us this evening that she sometimes has it on at night if she can't sleep and asked us to let her know if it ever disturbs us.

I stare at the wall dividing our two cottages.

Is that what it is?

That frisson again ...

I linger in front of the dying fire for a few more minutes, holding out my hands to ward off the unwelcome cold. My imagination is working overtime.

Eventually I climb the stairs, leaving Mittens to choose a chair to curl up on, while a multitude of thoughts and questions queue up in my mind for my attention.

Steve is fast asleep, snoring gently. In need of some warmth in the chilly bedroom, I tuck the duvet around my shoulders and give myself a hug. My sensible head has won. It's obvious. The voices Mittens and I had heard must've come from Joan's radio.

After all, what other sensible explanation can there be?

Chapter 13

A colourful stranger

Ellen
October 1880

Is that the grandfather clock's powerful tick I can hear? Or the pounding of my heart? I can't sort this out; it's beyond belief indeed.

Mother is getting ready to leave for home, unaware of what's happening outside. The rainy yard is giving way to such bright light that I have to shade my eyes. Powerful lamps on the walls light up the cottages; but what sort of lamps can they be? Where have they come from? They're not like any candle-lamps I've ever seen. The bleakness is being replaced with colour, a neatly trimmed grassy space is emerging, with a holly tree full of berries, and colourful curtains hang at each window.

Why have neither Matron nor Mother noticed anything unusual? Surely, I can't be the only one? The clock. It's so loud. A sudden dizziness threatens, and I hold on tight to the windowsill for fear I might fall and embarrass myself.

After several long, deep breaths I manage to calm down, and risk another glance up at the clock. It tells me it's six o'clock! How can that be, when it is, in truth, still early afternoon?

Back at the window, I rub my eyes frantically as I struggle to understand what I'm seeing.

I hardly dare move.

There is someone outside who, well, shouldn't be – visitors are not allowed to enter the yard unaccompanied. But this is no longer the yard I recognise. The gloom has been cast adrift, replaced by an unrelated world. The scene before me is beyond my ability to grasp.

There's a stranger, wearing the most luxuriant clothes ever owned by a common countrywoman; a bright red overcoat – the colour of rose hips – with a long blue dress peeping out below, and the daintiest of matching blue shoes, such as the likes of me could never hope to own.

She hurries across the grass, carrying a bunch of roses, but not the kind of roses I'm used to seeing in father's greenhouses. These are of every hue, never grown in any of our villager's gardens. Before I can get a closer look, she disappears into the light blazing from our open cottage door.

I am mystified.

My face feels warm, despite the chill of the office. I need to sit down and compose myself, to work out exactly what is going on out there.

I must mention nothing of this to Matron or Mother; it's clear they are oblivious to what's happening. And for some curious yet comforting reason, I am convinced that if I *did* dare to mention it, and they looked outside, neither of them would be privileged to see what I am seeing.

Matron peers up at the clock. It shows one o'clock, its hands now mysteriously rectified and its tick quietened. My shoulders slump with relief as the normal workhouse hour returns.

Mother has used up her allotted half an hour and it's time for me to get back to work in the kitchen, but it will be impossible to concentrate on my chores. We share one final cuddle, her cheeks cold and teary against mine.

She thanks Matron cordially before taking her leave.

I comfort her. "Don't be sad, Mother. Life in the house is … not as we'd feared. We're doing as well as could be hoped. Far better in fact."

She does her best to pull herself together before replying. "I could shed a bucketful of tears for you all, love, but how would that help? In the meantime, I have to say my eyes have been opened considerably about your situation here."

I am pleased to have eased Mother's misgivings about

life in the house. However, I am not about to cause her any further alarm by disclosing what I have witnessed in the yard.

Before leaving the office, she adds, "Once your Joe returns, things will get back to normal, no doubt about that. We must not lose hope."

No, we mustn't, but I wish I could share her faith that I'd see his dear face again before the next harvest is upon us.

Despite going over and over what had taken place in the yard, I manage to finish my kitchen duties, hugely heartened by the extraordinary experiences I've been privy to.

I'm intrigued by the *colourful stranger*. Part of me wants to accept that she is simply another rich visitor – that is the obvious conclusion. But the obvious is not always the case, is it? Something tells me there is far more to this than meets the eye.

Mother is not the only one whose eyes have been opened considerably today.

Chapter 14

Sad thoughts

Susie
October 2018

A whole month has passed since the move and my love affair with the cottage has gone from strength to strength. I love it all. Of course, it doesn't take long for Steve to point out we'll have to install double-glazing and do some re-decorating. He still hasn't got over his frustration at the repairer's failure to mend the clock and he constantly grumbles that there's barely enough space for a dining table for guests. But it doesn't matter what issues he might bring up: I'm not going to let him spoil my pleasure.

I'm starting to get to know some of the neighbours and it's easy to see how much they love living in their cottages, too. Joan, next door, has been living here for two years. She moved in as soon as the conversions were complete. And she adores her garden. I see her sweeping up leaves, pulling up the odd weed, even on a bitter cold day. I'll have to start showing an interest in *our* garden, or any weeds will spread their unwanted seeds into her borders – not good for neighbourly relations.

I'm hanging out the washing in the annex yard to take advantage of some welcome winter sun, when there she is on her path, wrapped up against the cold in her well-worn gardening anorak, scarf and hat, broom in her hand ready to sweep her path.

"You're busy this morning, Joan. You love it out here, don't you?"

She leans on her broom handle, puffs a bit, tugs off her gardening gloves and beams at me.

"Yes, I certainly do. I find nothing more satisfying than

creating a garden, and now I'm retired I can spend as much time out here as I like. I've been having a bit of a poke around to see what's coming up. Have you noticed your bulbs are starting to show their leaves, and my snowdrops are well on their way? The churchyard will be full of them, once Christmas is over. People come from miles around to admire their display, and before we know it, they'll be joined by primroses and daffodils."

I'm well out of my depth.

"Oh dear, I hadn't noticed the bulbs' leaves – you'll have to give me some lessons. Our last house had a large lawn with a patio and that was about it. I was teaching full-time and I'm afraid gardening didn't earn a slot on my weekend timetable: too busy planning lessons and catching up with housework."

"When did you stop teaching?"

Somehow, with Joan, I find I have no qualms talking about it. "I left work about six months ago, when I discovered I was pregnant. Sadly, extreme morning sickness meant I had to leave work sooner than I'd expected – teaching and feeling sick don't sit well together!"

Joan smiles. "And were you excited about being a mum?"

"Yes, I was thrilled. We'd practically given up hope of becoming parents, both coming up for forty, but having a child to care for was my dream." I choose not to add that it wasn't a dream Steve felt he could share.

"I planned to go back to work once my maternity leave was over; I'd made up my mind to try for a deputy head's position. At least, that was my aim …"

Joan bends down to pull out some more weeds, while I stare into space.

Teaching had meant everything to me. It became my solace. My class was like my family – I cared about every single child I taught. Their lively company helped me through many difficult times: days when I drove off to school at eight o'clock in the morning with hot tears streaming down my face, after Steve had treated me to one of his rants about nothing of any real importance. I always felt better after a few minutes in the classroom. My teaching friends convinced me I should go for a deputy head's job, and I would have, if things had been different.

I still miss the company of the children. No two days were ever the same. Every child was important; every child was special; I made sure of it, just as I'd hoped to make sure my own child would be special, one day.

Joan's voice brings me back to the present. "You're looking a bit wistful; are you feeling alright, Susie?" She tosses some weeds into the garden-refuse bag before giving me an enquiring glace.

"Oh, sorry – I was miles away. Just thinking."

"Sad thoughts?"

"Yes, 'fraid so." Despite my best efforts to keep them in check, the wretched tears won. "It was awful … We lost the baby."

Joan puts a warm hand on mine.

"How dreadful for you both, to have your hopes dashed."

"Yes, it was, and in my grief, I became seriously depressed." I'm picturing her, clear as day: the woman I turned into. I try to chase the image away.

I put on my positive face. "But eventually, I faced up to it and talked it through with my GP. I took the antidepressants and, as the weeks went by, a new, more positive phase began."

I look away.

Joan speaks gently, "And now you have a new home and a new garden to nurture."

There's a space in the conversation and somehow, in Joan's company, there is no need to fill it. I busy myself picking up a few dead leaves. If I'm honest with myself, I know what I ought to say, so I say it, bravely, "Yes … yes, I do."

I twist my wedding ring around my cold finger, a newly acquired habit since the move.

Chapter 15

'As sure as eggs is eggs'

Ellen
November 1880

It's time to ask Jane for her opinion.

After our six o'clock 'feast' of bread, a small portion of hard cheese and milky tea, Jane and I are enjoying a few minutes of well-earned rest in front of our meagre fire. The candle is alight, in the precious recreation time before the bedtime bell.

Once we've settled James and the girls into their beds and listened to their prayers, I'll have a chance to confide in her. I hope she might be able to help me sort out the recent curious events:

Who is the stranger I've seen in our yard?

How do bright lights shine from the cottages on occasion?

Is there a common sense explanation?

I sit down next to her. "Jane dear, I'd like to ask your opinion about some strange goings on in the yard. I'm hoping you can convince me that I'm not seeing – and hearing – things." I know I must say it. "*Things that aren't there.*"

She looks up from the newspaper and gives me a querying glance. "Go on …"

I begin. "Have you seen or heard anything out of the ordinary of late, in the house or out in the yard?"

She tilts her head and a quizzical frown appears.

I speak bravely, "Well, it's like this. When Mother was here yesterday, I was looking out of the office window to point out our lodging, when the most mystifying events occurred."

Jane folds up the newspaper and lays it on her lap.

"First of all, Master and Matron's grandfather clock began an ominous ticking, far louder than usual."

"What did Matron say?"

"She didn't say anything! Neither did Mother – because I'm sure they weren't hearing it."

Jane stares at me.

"Then, while the ticking filled the room, the entire scene outside altered before my eyes. The yard turned into a *garden,* such that Mother and I would love to own and nurture, with a neatly trimmed grassy patch and a holly tree filled with berries. All of a sudden it was early evening, and dazzling lights shone from each of these cottages, and gay curtains could be seen at the windows. And I know this is difficult to believe, but honestly, the clock – still ticking loudly – was clearly showing me *it was six o'clock*!"

Jane moves over to sit beside me on the wooden bench, taking hold of my hand. "Oh Ellen, whatever's the matter? Do you have a fever? Are you ill? Perhaps I should ask Matron to send for the doctor?" She smiles cheekily.

I grin back. "No, I'm not ill, but I must admit I did feel somewhat *ill at ease* at the time and I was concerned dizziness would overcome me and I would fall!"

Jane's face softens.

"But that's not all. As I watched, a stranger hurried across the grass towards our cottage, except it wasn't our cottage as we know it. There was a lamp on the outside wall, brighter than any we've ever seen, and similar lamps shone from some of the other cottages."

Jane shakes her head, very slowly. Is she about to dismiss my 'story'?

I'm keen to tell her everything. "And as for the stranger's clothes, they were most unusual. She was dressed in a truly vivacious, extravagant manner. She wore a long blue dress, as would befit a gentlewoman, under a rosehip-red overcoat. And she was carrying a bunch of roses, in many colours, the likes of which I have *never* seen, even in Father's glass houses."

Jane fails to suppress a chuckle. "Well, it's a puzzle where anyone could find roses in the workhouse, is it not?"

I give in to a giggle. "I know, a puzzle indeed! It was a swift sighting but there was no doubt about it, she was carrying the most eye-catching roses."

I allow myself a deep breath, preparing for Jane's reaction to my final revelation. "And please believe me when I tell you this, Jane: the more I think about it, the more convinced I am that she was," I lower my voice to a mere whisper, "*not of our time!*"

Jane pulls in her lips, striving to remain serious. "What do you mean, Ellen? *Not of our time*? Honestly; are you telling me that you think you were seeing a – *ghost*?"

I nod earnestly. "Well, either a ghost or *a real person*, from a time not lived in by us!"

Jane gets up, giving me a sympathetic smile. The warmth of her hand on my shoulder is comforting. "I know you're blessed with a profound imagination, but surely she was simply a well-dressed visitor who had mistakenly entered the yard without Matron's knowledge. Must have been."

I reply urgently, anxious that Jane will trust me to tell her the truth. "No, there is no question about it, she was no workhouse visitor. In fact, I could see that the transformed yard was only too familiar to her. After she'd disappeared into our cottage, I checked Matron's clock again, and to my relief it told the expected hour and was ticking normally once more. The delightful garden had merged back into our dingy yard."

We exchange glances.

"Strange to look back on it now, and most extraordinary to tell, but I'm sure she was visible to me *alone*. I'm certain of it. As you can imagine, I made no mention of what I'd seen to Mother or Matron; they would've been concerned and sent for the doctor, worried for the state of my mind. My instincts told me she would remain invisible to them." I'm getting out of breath. "There! Does this sound too silly for words?"

It's important to me that Jane will believe me, try to understand, but that can't be easy for her with only my extraordinary version to go on.

She's perplexed. I can tell she doesn't know what to make of me.

And to tell you the truth, neither do I.

I clasp her arm. "Dearest Jane, thank you for bearing with me, I do appreciate your patience, because I'd like to tell you about something else I've been seeing."

I twist my wedding ring around and around, gathering my strength.

"I've seen another puzzling inhabitant in the yard, as well as the stranger."

Her eyes are wide. "Another *puzzling inhabitant?*"

"Yes, Jane. I'm convinced we have a stray cat in the house. I know some would make fun of me if I told them, and say it was only a shadow, but they'd be wrong."

She bites her lip.

"The thing is, I keep seeing a black cat amongst the long grass by our step. The last time I saw it, it gazed up at me, purring persistently, as if it wanted to make friends."

Jane succumbs to her suppressed giggles. "You've been listening to old Alice, haven't you? Fills your head with all sorts of strange stories, she does. A black cat? Don't mention that to her, she won't like the sound of it one bit. She'll tell you it's an omen, a demon in disguise. She'll say it's been sent to warn you that evil spirits are waiting."

I put my hand over my mouth.

She goes on, "I recall how distraught she was last winter when she heard the screech of an owl. Gave her a terrible turn; wouldn't set foot outside her cottage after dark and Matron had to force her to do any work, even in daylight. Caused a great stir in the house, she did."

I take a more urgent tone. "No, Jane, this isn't some superstitious story put about by Alice. I'm serious about this. I'm in no doubt I saw the little cat; in fact, she's *not* black all over, she has the whitest of white paws. And I've given her a name. I've christened her 'Paws' because they show up so clearly in the darkness. I don't have to hear her meow to know she's about."

Jane's face softens.

"And as for her being an omen of evil spirits, there's no question of that. Quite the opposite in fact. I know she has come to *me, and me alone*, for a *positive* reason. But I do worry that if Matron catches sight of her, she'll shoo her away, or worse, ask the Master to put her out of her misery."

We sit in a friendly silence with our thoughts, staring into the fire. I'm grateful to Jane, she never tries to make me look foolish. She is content to let me have my 'imaginings', despite their incredulous nature.

She picks up the newspaper again. "If it will please you Ellen, I'll take you at your word. But don't mention what you think you've seen to anyone else or they'll be sure to poke fun of you, sure as eggs is eggs."

I persuade myself that it's not unusual to imagine creepy things in this place, especially once dusk has fallen. However, I have not altered my opinion. I had seen them both: the little black and white cat, and the colourful stranger in her rosehip-red coat. And seeing them has strengthened me. They aren't sinister in any way, quite the opposite – they bring a gleam of hope to lighten my darkness.

Meanwhile, Jane's advice rings true. My experiences must stay between the two of us for now. I have come to realise, over the years, that sometimes we have to take a risk, accept what our eyes and ears are telling us, and allow ourselves to experience what we could never have imagined.

But nevertheless, I must be careful. Jane knows what she's talking about; the others will be sure to poke fun if they hear about what I've seen, and cause alarm in the house – as sure as eggs is eggs.

Chapter 16

My flimsy explanation

Susie
December 2018

Joan and I are busy in our gardens, despite the cold, sweeping up the last of the autumn leaves. She puts down her broom and calls across to me. "I think it's time I stopped for a bit of a break and a warm-up. I'm going to make a pot of coffee. Would you like to join me? There's something I'd like to ask you."

A 'bit of a break' sounds good; my hands are cold, even in my gardening gloves.

Joan puffs a bit and rubs her aching back as we go indoors and take off our coats. I stand with my back towards her comforting Aga while we wait for the coffee to brew. I hope she'll be happy with 'Instant' when she comes round to mine. She sets out a plate of tempting biscuits, which she clearly didn't buy in Sainsbury's.

She smiles. "Still enjoying living here, Susie?"

"Oh yes, it's wonderful. Every morning, I gaze out at the smoking chimneys, the bare trees silhouetted against the sky, the blackbird perched in the holly tree and I get quite emotional. Does that sound silly?"

Joan laughs. "No, it's not silly at all; it's lovely. These cottages are special. Unique in fact."

It's curious she should use that word. It sums them up perfectly. Familiar goose bumps cover my arms for a few seconds, despite the warmth from the Aga. We sit down at her pine table in companionable silence for a moment or two, on chairs adorned with perfect patch-worked cushions, enjoying our coffee.

I put down my mug. "What was it you wanted to ask

me about, Joan?"

"Well, I hope you won't think I'm being nosy, but I wondered – were you and Steve away last weekend?"

"Yes, we were. We went up to London to visit my brother and his wife for the night, to take up their Christmas presents. Why do you ask?"

"Well, I thought you must have been going away when I saw Steve carrying a large hold-all down the path. I wouldn't have thought anymore about it, but later on, when it got dark, I noticed a flickering light upstairs in your cottage. Did you leave it on to ward off intruders, by any chance?"

"No … we didn't." A puzzled frown.

"Well, it was when I was wheeling in some logs from the garage after tea. As I trundled them up my path, something caught my attention at your bedroom window. There was, how can I describe it? A gentle glimmer, like a candle burning. But I knew it couldn't be a candle, if you were away."

I lean forward.

"And then there was the loud ticking."

I raise my eyebrows.

"Loud ticking, Joan? Are you sure?"

"Oh yes, you couldn't help but hear it. I knew your grandfather clock hasn't been working – you mentioned it at your housewarming – so it did bother me a bit. It was extremely loud."

I'm holding my breath.

"And later on, when I went up to bed, I heard – well – *voices.*"

I instinctively bite my bottom lip. "*Voices?* What sort of voices?"

So, Joan had heard them too. I breathe out, slowly.

She continues, "Oh – sounded like children reciting a poem, or possibly saying a prayer. And then they began to sing a Christmas carol. I recognized the tune."

"It must've been your radio, Joan. There's lots of Christmas music on at the moment."

She shakes her head. "No, Susie, my radio wasn't on. But don't worry, I wasn't exactly scared, more intrigued about how voices could be coming from your cottage when there was no one at home. In fact, I wondered if you'd left *your* radio on!"

I'm not sure if I should tell her that I'd been hearing them too.

"And as for your Mittens, she was sitting on the lawn, staring up, as if she could see something unusual at the window. You know how she flashes her tail about when she tries to see off a strange cat? Well, she was doing that, as well as sounding extremely excited – making that noise she makes when she spots a pigeon in my bird bath."

I gently touch her arm. "That's probably what it was, she'd seen a pigeon in your bird bath."

Oh my goodness – so it isn't only me. Joan had seen a candle burning in the cottage, and so had Mittens. I'd had my suspicions for a while now that she's been trying to alert me that something strange is happening, but I've been reluctant to allow myself to suspend disbelief.

As for hearing children's voices, carols being sung, and the extra loud ticking – I can't make head or tail of that. There's definitely something uncanny going on.

I do my best to reassure Joan, but I must admit, even *I* don't believe my flimsy explanation.

Chapter 17

Deck the halls

Ellen
Christmas 1880

I wake up, dog-tired.

I've been dreading the arrival of Christmas, ever since we were admitted, trying not to think about it. How will my boys cope, having Christmas away from home? We always tried the best we could to make it an extra special occasion for them. Am I foolish to hope that Christmas in the house could be a happy time?

In my darker, homesick hours, I picture the joys of Christmases past: Mother's special dinner of a rabbit from our village butcher – two if she could manage it – and all the vegetables proudly grown by Father and Joe. They would bring home a small fir tree from the estate, ready to be trimmed with ribbons, trinkets and the tiniest of candles. Henry helped Joe arrange sprigs of holly around the windows, tie mistletoe above the doorway and hang strings of ivy around the pictures. Both boys looked forward to finding sweets and an orange in their stockings on Christmas Day, although Henry tried to pretend he was much too grown up for such things.

I am very much afraid that such celebrations belong in a different world; a world we had left behind.

But now it's time – it can be put off no longer – we are facing Christmas *in the house.*

After all my misgivings, a few days before the 25th of December, there's a welcome surprise for everyone when the Master makes an announcement after breakfast.

"Good morning everyone."

He clears his throat; all eyes are fixed on him as he

continues. "I'm sure you'll be pleased to hear that you will not be required to do any hard work on Christmas Day or Boxing Day. It will be a holiday! Only the cooking and household chores will be carried out, as usual."

Broad smiles appear all round, and loud applause breaks out, as the men slap one another on the back, in high spirits. This is unexpected news, to put it mildly.

Jane and I will help with the Christmas dinner – an honour, not a chore – and when Matron informs us about exactly what we'll be cooking, our eyes grow wide, and our stomachs rumble.

She also tells us that extra family visits have been allocated for Christmas Eve. I'm looking forward to seeing Mother, to reassure her; she'll be bound to be concerned about how we will fare.

I'm on my way over to the office, where she'll be waiting, when I'm stopped in my tracks.

Loud ticking …

Across the yard …

I tremble, and not simply from the chill wintry air. A familiar aroma of mince pies baking starts to chase away the cold, making my mouth water. Tiny twinkling lights appear, strung high above the yard – or rather the *garden* – and music wafts out of the brightly lit cottage, such as I have never heard before.

And there she is again – my colourful stranger. I can see her clearly, through our downstairs window, standing in front of the prettiest of fir trees laden with dazzling glass baubles, such as only the gentry can afford. She's holding a wine glass in her hand and when she catches sight of me, she raises it high, like I've seen the squire's guests do. I struggle to hold back my tears, seeing the garden filled with light, while a full moon oversees proceedings, surrounded by frosty stars.

I stand still for what seems like many minutes but can only be but a few seconds, as the magical night-time garden slowly fades away and the dingy day-time yard reappears.

The music stops.

The clock is silent.

Reluctantly, I turn away, to set off for the office again, my happy tears drying in the December breeze.

*

Mother is beaming.

Matron has informed her that the Master is allowing us to have a break from our work for the two whole days of Christmas, news she is most heartened to hear.

I give her a hug and can hardly wait to put her in the picture about our Christmas fare.

"The guardians have been most charitable, Mother. Jane and I will be helping to produce a fine dinner of a good joint of roast beef and vegetables. And ... there'll be a pint of beer for all!"

She chuckles. "Roast beef, love? And beer? That sounds grand; somewhat different from our usual Christmas rabbit!"

I giggle. "And some of the guardians will be coming to watch us enjoy our meal at two o'clock tomorrow. What do you think about that!"

Her face glows.

Then she asks, "And will there be – by any chance – a Christmas pudding?"

I'm eager for Matron to hear my reply. "There certainly will! Matron and Master stirred up the mixture well in advance and it'll be simmering away in the morning. In fact, I understand they've made several, plenty to feed us all."

"I don't suppose you'll have a tree." She doesn't look at Matron, but she's swift to reply. "Oh yes, Mrs Freeborn, we have put up a handsome tree in the day room and the children have decorated it, with the help of some of the ladies from the estate."

Before we say goodbye and wish one another a Happy Christmas, she produces two stockings, filled with sweets and nuts, from her bag.

"For the boys, love. I want them to have the same as they had at home."

Matron turns towards her. "That's very thoughtful, Mrs Freeborn, but you needn't have worried. All the children will receive Christmas stockings filled with treats, kindly provided by the guardians."

Mother and I exchange satisfied glances, before she sets off on her wintry way once more.

Chapter 18

'Tis the season

Susie
Christmas 2018

Christmas has never been my favourite time of year. Whatever problems are happening in the family, you must be seen by everyone to be having a 'good time'. People become competitive about it, telling you how many Christmas cards they've sent, what amazing parties they've been invited to.

It was different when I was a child, carefree, believing that Father Christmas would come down the chimney with a sack of gifts and everything would be filled with fun and frivolity.

I guess it's all part of 'growing up'; coming to terms with inevitable Christmas family squabbles; arguing about who should be invited for the day or how much to spend on presents. When we were first married, I would get anxious about over-cooking the sprouts, under-cooking the pudding and what to do when uncle Jack got drunk …

*

This is our first Christmas in the cottage, enjoying the log-fire, watching the woodsmoke swirling outside with the mist in the air. It's Boxing Day and we've invited Kate and Graham for lunch, with our traditional cold meat and bubble and squeak menu, and they've just arrived when the phone rings. It's Joan.

"Susie, I'm so sorry to disturb you, I know you're having visitors for lunch, but …" she stammers, "it's George."

She'd been looking forward to having her brother spend Christmas with her this year, but now it's sadness that seeps down the phone. Her voice tapers off as she pauses to blow her nose. "He looks dreadful. I don't know what to do ... could you possibly ..."

I cut in, "I'm coming straight round, Joan. No worries, I'll be there in a sec."

"But what about your visitors? Have you had your lunch?"

"They'll be fine, don't you worry. It's all ready, all they need to do is dish up. They'll understand."

I know Kate and Graham will take charge of the food, no problem.

But I'm not prepared for Steve's reaction – or am I fibbing to myself again?

He stands up, thrusting his chair out of the way. "Trust you to find an excuse to spoil our Boxing Day, Susie! Surely Joan's perfectly capable of calling an ambulance? Why on earth do you have to go round there?"

Anger fuels my reply. "She's very upset, that's why! She needs a reassuring friend to wait with her. I'll follow the ambulance in the car. It's no problem, it's what friends do." I lose my patience. "But of course, that's something you seem to have forgotten about these days, Steve."

I'm beside myself with embarrassment that Kate and Graham have had to witness this outburst, especially at Christmas, but I know they would have done exactly the same for a neighbour in need.

I surprise myself at being able to face up to him, but it was well overdue.

*

Once George has been settled in a ward, I drive Joan home. I hoped she would spend the rest of the day with us, but she wants to stay in her cottage in case the hospital gets in touch.

Steve has disappeared to his den. I can't say I mind,

and I decide to open some wine to go with our warm mince pies. I fill our glasses, ready to sit down by the fire with Kate and Graham, to tell them how we got on at the hospital.

"I hope you had enough to eat, you two! I know how much Graham loves his bubble and squeak so I made plenty; you can take home the rest in a doggy bag if you like!"

We share a laugh.

I walk over to the window, glass in hand, with our Christmas tree behind me, and the curtains drawn back so we can enjoy the tiny Christmas lights twinkling on wires across the Square.

And then …

I glance over at Graham, and raise my eyebrows, but he simply looks puzzled, clearly unaware of the sudden loud ticking.

I gaze outside, pinching myself to make sure, but I'm certain there's someone out there, watching me through the window. I brush my sudden tears away as I instinctively raise my glass, in a Christmas toast, knowing that if I *should* venture outside all there'll be left to see will be our empty, magical moonlit garden.

Chapter 19

Bluebells

Susie
January 2019

I heard a blackbird singing this morning. He was perched on the roof-ridge opposite, silhouetted against a clear sky. His song filled me with hope and anticipation: a herald of spring, new life, new paths to follow.

I've decided it's time to start making a real effort with the garden. Never had the time or inspiration before, despite rattling around in our sterile house with a garden that could have looked attractive with a bit of work and knowhow, and more free time to devote to it.

Mrs Howard, the previous owner here, told me she would have loved to create a proper cottage garden, but as she got older her arthritis restricted her gardening activities. Now it's down to me to do the best I can.

I decide that the way to learn more about gardening is to ask an expert. I make a list of questions on my phone and drive the few miles to the local garden centre, my mind buzzing with ideas.

Luckily the outside plants section isn't too busy, and I manage to collar one of the staff. I can hear Steve's cynical voice in my head. *"Trust you to choose the blond, good-looking guy to help you. And my guess is, he'll be pretty fit under any wintry layers ..."*

But Steve isn't here, so my choice is my choice. And the *blond good-looking guy* willingly stops what he's doing and leans on his spade to listen.

I put down the wire basket. "I'm sorry to trouble you, I know you've got your work to do, but I wondered, can you spare me a minute or two, please? I'm looking for some advice."

He grins a flirty grin. "No problem, it's all part of the job, and anyway, I could do with a break. How can I help?"

I dig out my phone from my bag to look at my notes. "Well, we've recently moved into a cottage over in Hursley and I'd like to create a cottage-style garden from scratch. I can see the soil is chalky but apart from that, I'm a complete beginner. Can you show me where the chalk-loving plants are, please?"

I follow him around the displays, glad of my faithful red duffle coat in the struggling wintry sunshine.

He explains that many of the plants are dormant at this time of year, so I have a good look at the pictures on their labels to get an idea of how they'll look once spring arrives. My list is growing ...

Simon (yes, Steve, of course I asked him his name) points out some forget-me-nots and primrose plants. "You can't go wrong with these to start you off. They'll be in bloom before long and they come up each year. You could plant them in pots or tubs for now."

I soon pick up on his inspirational enthusiasm, a refreshing characteristic for me to discover in a man nowadays. Shrubs, perennials, annuals, bulbs – a lot to learn – and before long, with Simon's help, I'm loading several black plastic trays of plants into a trolley. The wire basket simply isn't up to the job.

Before I join the queue at the checkout, I impulsively add a gardening magazine to my shopping. This can't be more out of character. If my friends could see me, they'd burst out laughing. "Our Susie? Buying a *gardening* magazine? Who'd have thought it?"

It was the picture on the cover that caught my eye; it shows the most ethereal bluebell wood. Straight away it brought back childhood memories of going 'bluebelling' with my best school friend, in the Easter holidays. We'd ?le off down the lanes to the bluebell wood, hoping to ?ur bicycle baskets with lovingly gathered flowers, not a care in our world. As soon as I caught sight of the carpet of hazy blue, stretching away under the budding beech trees like a magical mist, I felt I could achieve anything so long as there were bluebells in my life.

Sadly, they never lasted long in their vases, but we still insisted on picking huge basketfuls around Easter Sunday, proudly presenting them to our mums and grandmas. I must admit I still can't resist picking wildflowers when I wander round the lanes, although I know I shouldn't.

It was my grandma who taught me all about the countryside. She took the time to show me how to press wildflowers and told me their names and their meanings, which I carefully pencilled in below each precious pressed flower in my exercise book.

And I still have it. I browse through it occasionally, pausing at the bluebell page, smiling to myself when I read my childish handwriting informing me that in Victorian times bluebells were known as a gift of gratitude.

And so, it has to be done – I grab six more plastic pots, ready-planted with bluebell bulbs, from a rack in front of the checkout and add them to my trolley.

Chapter 20

Rubbish

Ellen
January 1881

I cradle my aching head in my hands, lean on the edge of the icy cold kitchen sink and burst into tears. Matron is pacing up and down, treating me to one of her dreaded outbursts.

Unfortunately, I deserve it.

"How many times must you be told, you foolish girl?"

Shows how vexed she is, she can't bring herself to use my name like she normally does.

She yells, "We don't have money to throw away! You know how precious our medicines are; there are only three bottles of this cough syrup left. We do *not* tolerate breakages in the house; the Master takes a harsh view of any wastage, let alone the guardians."

I am fully aware that this accident is down to my carelessness. Matron had instructed me to return the bottle to its proper place in the medicine cupboard, once it was finished with. In truth, my thoughts are not on my tasks this morning; it's no wonder I knocked the wretched thing over.

Every ear in the kitchen is pricked. She hasn't finished.

"Stop all your other work for now and sweep up every single fragment of glass in case someone hurts themselves. Take the pieces to the heap at the end of the yard before the Master sees what you've done. You know the rules: all medicines are to be put away in the sickroom after use. No exceptions. How could you be so careless? You're neither use nor ornament to us today."

I carefully brush up the pieces of glass, wrap them in

newspaper and make haste outside to leave them on the rubbish heap, along with other broken jars and damaged china that Matron has put on one side to be thrown away.

Can this day get any worse?

Yet another dreary morning stretches ahead. Scrubbing the floors saps my energy. Matron always insists I must clean the kitchen floor daily, whether it is dirty or not. Today I will be obliged to scour extra thoroughly to remove every trace of the spilled cough syrup. Tears of exhaustion threaten, my curls hang limp with sweat and my head is throbbing.

I feel crushed by the weight of worry, in grave danger of giving up all hope for a better future. I try not to dwell on miserable matters, but it isn't easy. My wedding ring feels too big these days and as I twist it around my chilled finger. Loving thoughts of Joe fill my mind. With a heavy heart I pick up my scrubbing brush, rub it with smelly carbolic, and sink down on my knees to tackle the kitchen floor.

While I wait for it to dry, with the help of a cold breeze from the open doors and windows, I try to puzzle out, for the hundredth time, how I might earn a small living to help with the family income, once Joe returns and we are allowed to go home.

What are my skills?

And how can I make best use of them on the outside?

I could take in washing to help Mother, as I did before, but that won't suffice. It will be no easy task to make up for the loss of Father's and Joe's income.

Labouring at menial workhouse duties gives me plenty of time to puzzle things out, and after a great deal of heart-searching, I begin to think up a possible solution.

I will prepare myself to return to the work that *Father* taught me. Once Joe finds his new job, I will add my wages to his and Mother's, to ensure we can fend for ourselves. I will seek a position as a garden labourer on the Longmead estate, a position I believed God has always had in mind for me. I was truly devoted to my work there, in Father's Day.

He always used to say that if you have a trusted relative who's been employed up at the Big House, they'd welcome you in with open arms. I'll only have to mention Father and remind the squire of my years as his gardeners' boy, and he'll be more than willing to have me work for him again.

Sometimes, in my quiet moments, I try to imagine a time when a woman's skills will be respected, as a man's are. When all's said and done, why *shouldn't* a woman take up a position alongside a man? Some might say gardening is not fit work for women, but I don't agree. Yes, my wages will be half as much as a man would earn for doing the same work, and not sufficient to solely keep us, but we would manage – with Mother's laundry money, Joe's income and, if I have anything to do with it, my gardening pay.

That night, with sleep eluding me, my plan starts to grow. I wonder how the Master would react if I was bold enough to suggest starting a kitchen garden, here in the house. It would be a perfect way for me to enhance my skills and, at the same time, give fellow inmates a new purpose, for the little spare time they have. And, most important to the guardians, much of the expense of our food could be saved.

Out of the dreariness of the day's floor scrubbing, and the upset over the broken glass, a possible plan is emerging.

Chapter 21

Clues

Susie
February 2019

What I hadn't expected, working in the garden, was to start unearthing 'treasure', and it doesn't take long for my discoveries to mount up. While I'm having a bit of a tidy-up, I start to find fragments of blue and white china, oddments of crude crockery and chunks of thick blue and green glass.

One of the larger pieces of dark green glass has curious raised letters formed on it. I take it round to show Joan to see if she can shed some light; I'm wondering if she's found any in her garden.

I hand it to her and straight away her face lights up, "Oh! I know what this is, Susie! It's part of a Victorian medicine bottle. I've got some indoors that I dug up years ago. Come in and have a look."

I leave my muddy gardening shoes by her front step and pad into her kitchen in my socks. In the sitting room she shows me an interesting array of bottles and jars, displayed on her pine-dresser. She hands one to me, a dark green bottle with the raised words *'Not To Be Taken'* moulded into the glass.

She explains, "This bottle would've contained a strong medicine only to be taken on a doctor's say-so. The raised letters meant you could identify the contents if you were unable to read, or if it was dark, simply by running your fingers over the glass."

I feel the letters, and grin. "What a clever idea!"

She goes on, "I collected most of these when I was first married. A whole crowd of us used to go 'bottle digging', a popular hobby back in the late sixties. There was a bottle shop in Southampton where you could take them to sell, or perhaps buy more for your collection."

My toes are tingling.

"We never knew what we'd unearth, which was what made it so much fun. We found all sorts – medicine bottles, Bovril bottles, marmalade jars, mustard pots and beer bottles. The best place to find them was under patches of nettles on what used to be nineteenth-century rubbish tips, on waste ground."

My mind is working overtime.

"You see them on sale these days at antique fairs and car-boot sales; collectors queue up for the rarer ones."

So – the previous inhabitants of these cottages had left broken china and glass on their rubbish heap, and that's what I'd been unearthing. Joan has more than aroused my curiosity.

I say, "Well, I can't wait to start digging again! I'll let you know if I find any more."

Back in our garden I contemplate the rough patch where my treasures had been hiding, and I wonder: I wonder about the people who lived here before the cottages became derelict, who might have thrown away those broken bottles and pieces of china.

Whenever I walk into a church, or perhaps along a well-trodden cobbled street, I try to picture who may once have walked where I'm walking. Seeing Joan's bottles has me well and truly hooked. How did those previous occupants spend their days? If only I could meet them and hear their stories. I can't wait to investigate.

*

August 2019
Looking at Joan's bottle collection inspired me: since then I've kept an eye open for them at antique markets and junk shops. My collection is growing: it's become a fascination.
  And it keeps me close to her.

Chapter 22

Where no child lives

Ellen
February 1881

There is no longer any doubt, I am the only inmate privileged to see Paws.

I catch sight of her most days. She is certainly no illusion, and she has the ability to enhance my life in immeasurable ways. She crouches down in the yard in front of me as a matter of course now, before rubbing against my legs, looking for a fuss. She gazes up into my face, purring, knowing I'll have saved her some scraps when I cleared the plates after dinner, to leave them where she can smell them, in the long grass outside our door.

Sometimes, when I bend down to smooth her, I see a now familiar colourful figure through our parlour window. There is no longer any mystery about who she is and what she is doing here. The stranger in the rosehip-red coat, who I'd seen in the garden carrying the roses, and enjoying her glass of wine at Christmas, is an *ally,* who's travelled to my workhouse world to support me in a way I have yet to discover. Seeing her makes me feel safe and cared for.

On the other hand, if I am right, and she *is* from another time, how can that possibly be? My mind finds it overwhelming, trying to cope with the idea of a visitor *from another world, in another time, not lived in by me.*

Am I suffering from delusions?

*

I heard a robin singing as we dressed in the darkness this morning. The sharpness of his song filled my head with mournful longings for my Joe, and pitiful tears pricked my eyes. How much longer must we wait for his return?

Before getting down to work, I linger in the yard for a few more minutes, to listen to the loud, gathering rooks cawing and circling. I've been told by fellow inmates that before long they'll be taking up residence high in the towering beech tree over in the churchyard opposite the end of this lane, heralding the arrival of spring.

How I long for our freedom – to be able to go for a walk whenever and wherever I wish, to wander the lanes on a whim to search for early snowdrops, and later on for primroses, but most of all, to rest from my chores whenever I'm over-tired. But, for now, I can only hide away my longings and wend my weary way to the steamy, sweaty laundry room where mounds of miserable mangling are waiting.

As I cross the yard, I am puzzled by the sounds of children, squealing and shrieking outside the end cottage on our side, a cottage *where no child lives.*

I stand perfectly still to listen – to make sure – but no, I must have been mistaken. It's only the cries of the rooks, soaring overhead. I glance over once more, to check if there *are* any children outside, and I can't help but feel smug, as the distinct movements and sounds of children scuttling indoors reward me.

Over in the churchyard, the rooks continue their unmistakable cries.

Chapter 23

Rooks

Susie
February 2019

Steve nearly throws a fit when I tell him a family with children will be moving into the Square. He instantly goes into moan mode. He still doesn't enjoy the company of children; he says he feels out of place. I'm the opposite; I love to hear children playing. It reminds me of my teaching days doing playground duty. To me it's a comforting sound, even if it is second-hand.

Joan had mentioned that a young family would soon be moving into the cottage at the far end of the terrace. Steve and I are in the kitchen having a coffee when we spot their removal van draw up at the gate.

He glares out of the window. "Oh no! They're here! A family with a clutch of noisy kids! That's all I need. Bang goes any chance of peace and quiet. How can I be expected to concentrate on my work with their rumpus to contend with?"

I'm furious. "Don't be so mean! It's about time you learnt to be more tolerant with children. They're excited about their new home, that's all. It's natural."

I hear them squealing and shrieking as they kick a ball about in their new garden. I don't have a problem with any of it – they're simply having fun.

*

I've started to make progress with the garden. Slowly. And yes, Grandma, you'll be pleased to hear I am actually enjoying it.

My grandma wasn't only a self-taught wildflower 'expert', she was also a keen gardener. She'd tried to encourage me to take an interest, as a child. Any chance she got she'd be pottering about amongst her plants, tugging at weeds, dividing up clumps of flowering plants to share with neighbours, or filling up her mossy metal watering can after a hot day.

She'd pop outside to hang out her washing – *"I won't be a minute, love!"* – and take forever to come back indoors, nosing about to see how her plants were thriving, clutching her empty washing basket and peg bag as she went. Mum and I used to tease her about it. How thrilled she'd be to know that I'm taking after her at last.

Following Simon's advice, I've planted young lavender plants to make a low hedge each side of our path, and forget-me-nots and primroses have claimed their places in terracotta pots, as he'd suggested, ready to cheer up the front doorstep now that spring is not too far away.

I chose the perfect place for the bluebell bulbs, next to the clump of grass by the back doorstep. I'll be able to enjoy their familiar sight and perfume every time I open the kitchen door, once May is here.

The more time I spend in the garden the more I find solace in it, losing track of time, and I particularly love to hear the raucous clatter of the rooks. They're gathering above the ancient beech tree over in the churchyard, sprinkling the sky with their signature shapes. I lose track of time as I watch them, revelling in their calls as they soar overhead,

"Don't you realise it's almost lunch time?" Steve grumbles, without fail, if I take a long time to come in.

Being outdoors in the fresh air lifts my spirits, and I enjoy the garden on cold days too, if I'm well wrapped up. At long last I *get* it. I understood how nurturing plants can be therapeutic; for me it helps satisfy my redundant caring instincts. And, as I'd hoped, my habitual tears have begun to slide into the background since the move. In fact, I've made a point of pouring them into a jar, to hide them at the back of my wardrobe.

Working in the garden never feels like a chore: it's a delight. It's easy to put aside my past sadness and focus solely on caring for my plants. It sometimes puzzles me why I'd never taken more of an interest in our old garden, but when I stop to think about it, the reason is obvious. I've been waiting for the *right* garden to take an interest in *me*.

Over in the church yard, the rooks circle again, filling the air with their distinctive cries.

*

After my conversation with Joan about her bottle collection, researching the history of the cottages is next on my list. I know Graham will have some suggestions to get me going so I give him a ring before I start cooking supper.

As I dial his number, my fingers tingle …

"Hi, Graham, it's Susie."

"Susie! How's it going? I hear from Kate you're turning into a bit of a gardener. Doesn't sound like the Susie we know and love!"

I smile. "It's going well, Graham. The cottage is pretty much sorted, and as for the garden, well, it's caught hold of me; I feel it tempting me, wanting to reveal its secrets." I can't help blushing. "I expect that sounds a bit silly."

"No, it doesn't, it sounds great. Do you good to have a fresh project on the go."

They never mention it unless I bring it up, but he and Kate are well aware of how I've been feeling these past six months, despite putting on a brave face in front of them.

I curl up on the sofa, to talk to him.

"The thing is, I've been unearthing 'treasure' in the borders when I'm weeding – pieces of broken glass and china. I showed them to Joan, and she explained that back in the sixties, she and her friends used to dig for bottles and jars on what were once *Victorian rubbish heaps!* I'm thinking there could have been one here, in this garden."

I picture Graham's supportive smile.

"I'm inspired to find out about the people who lived here and threw away their broken glass and china. With all the family history research you've done, I thought you'd be the perfect person to ask."

I can hear Graham's enthusiasm. "I'd start with the builders if I were you. Why not give them a ring? They'll know as much as anyone and you can take it from there. And call me anytime if you'd like more guidance."

I'm picking up a Biro to make a note of the builders' number when an unexpected movement in the increasing gloom outside catches my attention. What on earth's going on? Darkness has fallen, far too early, as if someone has switched off the sun, replacing it with ominous clouds. Could there be a thunderstorm threatening?

I frown.

Our poor broken clock is ticking again – a loud, slow warning. I open the door on the front of its case, just to check, and catch my breath. The pendulum is swinging away.

Strongly. Not broken at all.

I close my eyes, frantically turning my wedding ring. I bite my bottom lip.

Premature darkness?

Candles?

Bare windows?

Our broken clock coming to life?

I shiver.

The path is spotted with raindrops and there's hardly a light to be seen, the blackness only relieved by stubby candles guttering at bare windows. It's impossible to see anything with clarity. In the last few minutes time has lost its way.

A rain-spattered Mittens trots towards the cottage, apparently unperturbed by the untimely arrival of nightfall. The garden is almost fully dark. How is that even possible? I can barely make out the shapes of the holly tree or Joan's birdbath.

And there's someone I don't recognise, in the damp darkness, walking slowly towards Mittens. A young, extremely slim – or should I say thin – woman with longish curly hair, and an old-fashioned air about her has emerged out of the gloom. As she comes nearer, I can see she's wearing a wintry grey skirt down to her ankles, with a long red petticoat showing below, and vintage-style black laced boots.

A long petticoat?

Who on earth wears a long petticoat *in 2019?*

Mittens is confidently rubbing around her legs, not timidly like she normally is with strangers; this woman is no stranger to her. When she reaches the grassy patch near the kitchen door, she pauses, stoops down, and carefully places something amongst the grass.

I watch them in the shadows, through the sitting room window, with the phone still in my hand. "Sorry Graham; got to go. There's someone outside. I'll call you back," and I put the phone down.

By the time I open the door to say hello, it's too late – she's nowhere to be seen. I dash outside into the dissolving darkness, where the rain is gradually easing off and the porch light is heroically doing its job again. I peer around the garden, before hurrying out of the gate to scan up and down the lane, but there's no sign of her.

As I close the front door behind me, my mind is overwhelmed with baffling images – unexplained rainy darkness, guttering candles, a broken clock that isn't broken, and a curious young woman, who looks as if she's stepped out of a Victorian novel.

Only Mittens is left, blinking, at where her friendly visitor has been. She settles down to enjoy her food amongst the straggly grass, where until a few minutes ago, there was no food at all.

Chapter 24

Ghosts?

Susie
February 2019

I take Graham's advice and give the builders a ring.

They tell me these cottages were once the area's workhouse, in the late eighteen-hundreds. I can hardly get my head around it – Steve and I are living in a *workhouse*!

Hmmm. I know precisely what he'll have to say about that.

Here is a subject I know next to nothing about, so I'm fascinated to find plenty of facts online. In no time, my mind is teeming with images, ideas and questions.

Perhaps exploring those unfortunate people's lives, played out here in the last century, can help me sort out my own life. Not only discovering what everyday life was like for them, but how they *coped*; how they dealt with sadness and hopelessness; how they stayed sane in such a place.

There is so much I want to discover. How did they come to be living in the workhouse in the first place? What about their children? Did they live there too? And were they ever able to leave?

It amazes me how anyone found out about anything before we had the internet. All you have to do is Google a subject and there'll be more information than you could ever hope to find, and the workhouse websites are no exception. Sorting out this real-life historical jigsaw puzzle is proving to be irresistible.

Piece by piece a picture is beginning to come together, showing what life was like for the Victorian residents of 'The Square'. It must have been the inmates who discarded my garden treasures on their rubbish heap. Must have. It's all starting to make sense.

Steve's face is a picture when I tell him what the builders have said.

"Really? A *workhouse*? Well, all I can say is, it can't have been very big, can it? I thought workhouses were notoriously huge, imposing institutions. There're only the two rows of cottages here, and the annex. How did that work, I wonder?"

"Yes, I know, that's what I thought. But here's the thing. I've discovered online that not every Victorian workhouse was huge. We only imagine they were. Some were vast, especially near the towns, but there were many others that weren't, and Hursley was one of the smaller ones."

Steve heads for the back door. "Okay, I can see why you find it interesting, but don't get too caught up. You know what you're like with your vivid imagination; before you know where you are, you'll start believing you're seeing the *ghost of a workhouse inmate*!"

He wanders off across the garden to his den, laughing at what he thinks is a joke.

Little does he know he's quite right.

I *do* believe I've seen a ghost – but it isn't a joke.

Not a joke at all.

*

It's time to look at the census.

I rub my hands; they feel cold despite the heating being on, nerves taking their toll. This search could provide the answer to many of my questions.

Local history had never been my thing until we moved here, but let's face it, this is a completely new scenario for me. This is history that took place *here, in this very cottage*. I'm about to read an *actual* census return for this workhouse *in 1881, one-hundred-and-thirty-eight years ago.*

Mind blowing.

I fire up my laptop and soon have the census on the screen. My mouth is dry as I try to prepare myself. I'm about to lift the lid of a long-buried treasure chest and I'm almost too frightened to peer inside, in case it's full of disappointment.

I lean forward in my office chair to examine the screen and, oh my word, there they are! The 'inmates' who lived here in 1881. Yes, *inmates:* that's what they were called. It sounds unfeeling, as if they were prisoners, which I suppose in a sad way they were.

The census also shows where they lived before they came into the workhouse, their occupation, if any, and their ages.

I manage to make myself calm down, taking a few deep breaths before carefully scanning the list, reading the names and details of the female inmates. There are only two young women listed and there is one name that jumps out at me.

My fingers shake as I move the mouse.

There she is.

Now I can give my friend from the past a name; her name is Ellen, Ellen Martin, and she was thirty-four years old, living in this workhouse in 1881, with her two boys, Henry age twelve and James age four.

I sit back, hardly able to take it in, looking up at the ceiling to let out the long breath I was unaware of holding on to.

Ellen, the young Victorian woman, is real.

My mind is not playing tricks.

I haven't invented her. I've been seeing her, in her environment, one-hundred-and-thirty-eight years ago.

I have travelled to her time.

The hairs on my neck tremble.

This census return lists *real* people who walked where *I* walk, lived where *I* live and who worked unceasingly, in dire conditions, with no other choice from all I'd read online, *in these cottages.* I am privileged to share a closeness to them – well, to one in particular – and I believe I'm involved in this whole 'other world' experience for a significant reason I've yet to uncover.

I rest my head on my hands for a minute. What if our cottage turns out to be *her* cottage? Each room would take on a new personality for me. I could be sitting in *Ellen's bedroom*, she could have looked out of *this* window and walked down *these* stairs.

As I try to absorb what I've learnt, it all starts again – I can hear the untimely, unnaturally loud ticking from downstairs as, imperceptibly, darkness has descended, and stubby candles are appearing, one by one, through bare windows. I tug my warm jumper sleeves over my cold hands as I watch our garden fade away to become the workhouse yard once more, barely lit, bleak and barren.

I don't know what to do with myself.

Mittens is on the path, washing her perfectly clean white paws and her perfectly clean white bib, in the growing darkness. Next moment she's dashing around, skittish, expectant.

And there she is – *my Ellen*, for that's what I will call her now – standing in the half light, wearing her long, grey woollen skirt with her red petticoat like before, and today she's added a warm-looking blue and white striped shawl to fend off the night time's chill.

I can't take my eyes off her.

She has something in her hand. Mittens scampers up, trotting along the yard beside her, tail in the air, looking up at her face. Ellen heads for the long grass where I'd been working earlier.

Little by little, the lawn resumes its rightful place, the holly tree reappears, and our sundial shows its face. Low background traffic noise from the main road signals the return to the twenty-first century, light replaces the gloom, the porch lamp is back on, and Ellen is no longer in her yard: she's here, *in our garden.*

I have to pinch myself to make sure I'm not in the middle of a daydream. But there is absolutely no question about it, she can see me just as I can see her.

And there is only one way to explain it, *Ellen and I have both travelled through time.*

There.

I'd said it.

Out loud.

A concept too epic for either of us to grasp, let alone understand.

She glances up at this window, and smiles a shy smile, her eyes shining in her pasty face. I quiver with anticipation, move closer to the window and return her smile. I risk a friendly wave, and, to my delight, she timidly waves back, before she stoops to place some food in Mittens' grassy corner, like before. The cat waits, white whiskers twitching, and as soon as she gets the chance, she squeezes herself around Ellen's legs to find her food.

Once she's finished eating, she laps from a convenient puddle before disappearing indoors, through the cat flap. Ellen watches, rooted to the spot, as the tantalising tip of the cat's tail slides slowly through, and the flap mysteriously clatters shut behind her.

Ellen remains where she is for a bit, looking puzzled, no doubt trying to work out how and where the cat has gone. Finally, she wipes her hands on her apron, and strolls back the way she came. When she passes Steve's annex door, she turns around, looking back at this window, as if checking I'm still here before walking away. As she leaves, she loses all colour, like a photograph left out too long in the sun.

I'm beside myself. Such a lot to take on board: my friend from the past has a name; I can watch her in her workhouse yard and in our garden. And she can watch me.

We'd communicated, with smiles and waves.

I stare, unseeing, into the space Ellen has left, for several minutes, itching to uncover the reason I'm seeing her in her world.

Looking beyond the obvious is the key for me. I've learnt there's nearly always a hidden story to be found – if you're prepared to take the time to look – and I can't wait to explore this one further.

Is this the cottage she lived in?

And if it is, did she ever sit where I'm sitting?

And, the most important questions of all for me: does she die in the workhouse? Or does she leave?

*

I remember a night, before we moved here, when we had a power cut and I couldn't recall where I'd put the emergency candles. Our house was in pitch darkness; I literally couldn't see my hand when I held it close to my face, and even with a lighted candle it would've been tricky to find my way downstairs.

Whenever I light a scented candle as a treat, I ponder once more about the lives of those unfortunate inmates. My candles are purely for decoration and fragrance but theirs provided the only light they had, apart from firelight.

Ellen lived her workhouse life in darkness, dreariness and despair. In the winter months she would have risen in the dark, before dawn, only to return, in the dark, at the end of her daunting day.

Do I honestly believe I can help her?

Or will my common sense prevail?

Chapter 25

Whatever next?

Susie
February 2019

It's Saturday morning and I'm busy in the garden again, as the forecast is good. Everything's starting to take shape. I've made several more visits to the garden centre and they're paying off; the lovely Simon keeps an eye out for me and usually has a new plant or two for my inspection.

I'm wrapped up warm in my old fleece sweater and jogging bottoms, loving being outside, despite it only being February. Two of my primrose plants are bravely blooming, the forget-me-nots look promising and the bluebell bulbs are getting ready under the soil, waiting to show off their leaves outside our kitchen door in the sunny corner.

I decide to sort out the large patch of dishevelled grass once and for all. It's got out of hand after the rain we'd had, and a major tidy is called for. I'm careful not to cut it too short or I'll get into trouble with Mittens. She loves it. Whenever the sun is out, even a white wintry one, this sheltered corner gets quite warm. It has become her favourite spot, especially since she's started finding regular food treats.

Graham has driven over for a chat with us both. Good excuse for me to stop work and make a coffee. The three of us squat on the kitchen doorstep, lifting our faces to the welcome burst of wintry sunshine and warming our hands around our steaming mugs.

"Still intrigued with your findings, Susie?" Graham munches on a chocolate digestive. "What've you found out so far?"

Steve's face stays closed, while mine is wreathed in enthusiastic smiles. "Oh, it's absolutely fascinating. After I spoke to the builders and they told me these cottages were once part of a workhouse, I started looking for information online."

Steve peers over his glasses, reaching for another biscuit.

I put down my coffee. "It's all there, in the eighteen eighty-one census. It turns out that this particular workhouse wasn't anything like we all imagine a workhouse to be. It was tiny, one of the smallest in the county in fact, with thirty-five inmates and, how about this? With a *'kind hearted Master and Matron'* in charge! I hadn't expected to find that sort of detail. I read the official report written at the time, after an inspection by the Lancet Commission."

Graham's eyes twinkle. "I wouldn't have expected that, either. I'd have thought they'd be harsh disciplinarians, hated by the inmates. Wasn't that their job? I thought living in the workhouse was meant to be a deterrent, to keep malingerers out."

"I know. I think that was usually the case, but they wrote positively, referring to the Matron here as *'cheery and kind and with a warm heart',* and describing the Master as *'a friend and protector to all.'* This workhouse might have been tiny, but it was kindly managed and not nearly as dreadful as most workhouses were."

Graham grins at the thought. "There are often exceptions to a preconceived idea, aren't there? Things can turn out quite differently from what you expect."

I continue, "And how about this? They were usually built at the edges of towns, or out in the villages, because no one wanted to live near a workhouse. There was a huge stigma about it, unsurprisingly."

I'm in full flow. It was a rare treat to talk to someone who shared my enthusiasm. "This little place was different in every way from an urban workhouse, which could house hundreds. Thousands sometimes. People were terrified of going in, because they'd have heard the scary stories."

Graham has picked up on Steve's distinct lack of interest, and gives me a sympathetic hug, and we watch him disappear into the kitchen, ostensibly to make us all another coffee.

"Sounds as if most of them were pretty grim, to say the least."

I nod. "Yes, grim is the word. Mind you, I don't doubt it was bare, cold and damp here, and the food would have been plain, with not a lot of it, but I've read nothing about ill treatment or abuse in this workhouse, as there was in some apparently. Quite the opposite in fact."

Graham smiles.

"And how about this? The report says that after the Master and Matron were highly praised by the inspectors, they were awarded a special gift from the wealthy Hursley guardians in recognition of their years of invaluable service."

I'm already wondering what that 'special gift' might have been.

"Wouldn't living in a workhouse have been like living in a prison?" Graham stands up to take a good look around what would've been the workhouse yard.

"Well, I guess it was a bit like that, but you could ask to be let out to search for work or to go to the village church, so long as you returned at the time you were told. Your sole *crime* was being poor and unable to support yourself; you were free to leave once you found employment, but that wasn't easy. The saddest part was, you were separated from your older children, and your wife or husband."

Graham grins. "And now, here you are, one-hundred-and-thirty-eight years later, planting flowers where there was once a bare yard, and finding treasures! Whatever next, I wonder?"

Whatever next indeed.
*

Once Graham has driven away, I'm back in front of my

laptop, with a dry mouth. This next search is crucial; so much depends on what it reveals, and it doesn't take long to find what I'm looking for.

Here it is: the 1891 census, ten years after the last one, with the workhouse inmates listed, as before. I close my eyes for a few seconds, holding my breath, preparing myself for what I could be about to learn.

I scan carefully up and down the screen several times to check, *but there is no Ellen Martin listed.*

She was not living here in 1891.

There is no Henry or James mentioned either.

They had all left the workhouse.

I look away from the computer, waiting for my heartbeat to slow down.

Before I get too carried away, I must think about this sensibly – if she wasn't listed in the census, it doesn't necessarily mean she found a way to leave the house. Perhaps she died in those ten years? Or had her boys found outside employment?

Of course, I know what I *want* to be the case: that she *didn't* die here but found a way to leave and took her boys with her. And, most important of all, I believe that I have a part to play in helping her to do it.

It couldn't be clearer to me now, why I was enticed into moving here, to travel to her world, to observe her life in the workhouse, to share the emotions of a young Victorian mother who *took the house* because she had no other choice.

What is becoming unquestionable to me, day by day, through helping her, is my belief that new doors will open, and a new life will begin …

For both of us.

Chapter 26

A touch of luxury

Susie
February 2019

I love to lie in the warmth of the bath, sometimes enjoying a glass of wine, and daydream, making plans for exotic holidays, new ventures. So, it's not a surprise when I come up with a plan for Ellen this evening.

Once the warmth and fragrance of the water has helped me relax, I think over various bath-time musings I've had through the years – to apply for a deputy headship, to be more decisive with Steve and stand up for myself, to be honest about our crumbling marriage. Sadly, I'd yet to find the confidence to take the necessary steps to make those ideas a reality. I'd foolishly let my plans stay in the bathroom, doomed to merge with the steam and disappear into thin air.

But tonight, things are different.

I relax amongst the bubbles and try to picture what bath time would have been like for Ellen and the other women in the workhouse.

I'd read they were only allowed a bath once a week, often supervised, in tepid, shallow water, using carbolic soap, notoriously difficult to lather. It's hard to know how that must have felt, to be so humiliated and disrespected.

If I'm serious about trying to help Ellen, I must think of a way to make solid contact with her, without scaring her. I want her to see me as a kindly presence: *a friend;* the last thing I want to do is frighten her away. She must have all sorts of concerns about who she is seeing, as I did when I saw her for the first time.

Now that we've exchanged smiles and waves, and she's

made friends with Mittens, I decide my next step will be to leave her some tangible evidence that I'm *real* and can be trusted to do her no harm.

The best thing I can do is to leave her a tangible sign, possibly a gift to enhance her life, something she could keep to herself. It must be something familiar – something she would recognise – yet never expect to find in the workhouse. I must choose something small, that she could hide away from prying eyes, and not risk having it confiscated by the Matron.

I bundle myself up in my fluffy white bath towel, still warm from the airing cupboard, and as I put away my bottle of bubble bath, it comes to me.

What has every woman appreciated, since time immemorial?

A touch of luxury.

And I've got just the thing.

She'll love it.

A bar of lavender soap that I keep to scent my dressing table drawer. It was a birthday gift from Grandma. I'll leave it on the step tomorrow, for my Victorian friend to find when she returns to the cottage after her supper.

Downstairs I curl up on the sofa in front of the fire, to think this all through.

By myself.

Steve will do what he always does these days: work in his den until late and leave me to enjoy my own company. Not a problem; that suits me fine. I'll make the most of the uninterrupted time to work out the details.

I can hardly wait for morning.

Chapter 27

To be so cherished

Ellen
February 1881

We enjoy the stewed mutton and carrots for our dinner, with scant portions of vegetable soup and three-day-old bread for supper, but it leaves us still hungry, as usual. It's my turn to clear away the plates; a perfect chance to salvage a few morsels of meat to leave later for my Paws.

How the day is dragging its feet, every task feels as if it will take forever. The drizzle only serves to further dampen my spirits, if that's possible, and I long for my bed. It'll be early to sleep for all of us tonight, as soon as I've fed little Paws.

I search around the yard but there's no sign of her. I wander alongside the wet grass to leave her food and suddenly I spot something: something that ... shouldn't be there.

Something that doesn't belong but is truly beguiling.

I wonder ... What is the most meaningful gift you've ever received?

Something small?

Something extravagant?

My colourful stranger knew exactly what I would love. How could I resist it? It's tantalising, precious and meaningful. Yes, it's a bar of soap, but with a singular hue. It is the colour of lavender, a gentle blue, with an unmistakable matching aroma. Straight away, it brings thoughts of Mother, and how much she adores lavender. She loves looking after the few lavender bushes she's planted by our garden path.

How she would have delighted in the luxury of scented

soap, but with a family to feed she was obliged to choose between purchasing a much coveted, but expensive, perfumed bar of soap, or a good joint of beef to provide our family with several nourishing meals. Carbolic was all she could afford. We were only too aware that luxuries like scented soap were reserved for the gentry; certainly never for the likes of us.

I pick up the soap, carefully, hold it to my nose, and my cheeks warm as its fragrance floats around me. I shut my eyes, breathing its soothing scent.

And, all at once, I feel *special*, for the first time since we entered the house.

Like a lady.

There's not a soul about in the rainy yard, but I keep my eyes peeled, in case someone appears, catches the aroma and becomes curious. I will never dare to use it, or keep it about my person, for fear its scent will draw attention and Matron will whisk it away. I must keep it hidden, away from prying eyes. It perfumes my fingers delightfully, bearing no resemblance to any soap I have ever used.

However much I struggle to explain it, I can find no other sensible interpretation: my colourful stranger has left me this gift, as a sign of her presence – and her goodwill.

I risk a glance up at the bedroom window, now adorned with blue patterned curtains, and I'm rewarded with the sight of her again, watching. Brightness streams around the yard, lighting up the wet path. She waves, cautiously, and I wave in return, tears of gratitude pricking my eyes.

I am utterly overcome: to be so cherished by a kindly benefactor, who has chosen not only to travel to find me, but now to leave this precious gift, from her mysterious colourful world.

Before I can stop myself, I start to twirl around and around in the rain, filled with wonder that such a thing should happen to me.

Finally, I pause, to risk one more precious glance up at her window, but the brightness has faded and all there is left to see is the bare, black, rain-spotted window of our workhouse bedroom.

*

Summer 1911

It wasn't until she left me the soap, that I experienced how it felt to dance for joy. I couldn't help myself; nothing could mar my gaiety.

And my life has continued to feel joyful.

'However did that happen?' I hear you ask.

My answer has to be, 'It happened because I chose to believe in the unbelievable.'

Chapter 28

A hint of lavender

Susie
February 2019

All set.

The broken clock is ticking. It tells me it's seven o'clock, and the garden has once again changed its persona. It is bare of greenery, shrouded in drizzly darkness, with only one or two candle stubs flickering at bleak windows. No porch light, no lawn, no holly tree.

My Ellen is dragging herself towards the cottage. I catch my breath as she gets nearer, her poor thin body swamped in her ill-fitting workhouse clothes. Despite her exhaustion from another day's dreary work, she's finding the time to hunt around in the darkness for Mittens.

She takes the precious scraps of food from her apron pocket and is about to put them down in the rain-soaked grass, when she hesitates, clearly perplexed. After a moment or two, curiosity gets the better of her and she reaches down to pick up my gift. She is dubious to start with, not quite understanding what she's found, but once she's studied it, she straightens up, lifts the soap to her nose with both hands and closes her eyes, revelling in its lavender scent.

Her face is wary as she scans the yard before shyly looking up at this window. She's looking for me. She knows exactly where her gift has come from.

I don't hesitate. I wave through the rain-spattered glass and she bravely returns the gesture. We are both wiping away our tears, when all at once her careworn face lights up; she is in no doubt. She *knows* I left the soap for her. She gazes in wonder at it before holding it close.

I could never have predicted what she does next; to my amazement, she begins to dance – a heart-wrenching twirl of child-like excitement – before disappearing into the darkness once more.

*

August 2019

Every time I saw Ellen, it felt magical. Unique. How many of us get the chance to visit the past – in the present?

Seeing how she reacted to finding the soap showed me that whatever time we live in, we experience the same emotions – pleasure and pain, happiness and despair, and, yes, pure joy. Events change us, give new insights, strengthen us, and as a result enable us to solve our problems.

I wonder how long she kept my gift.

I doubt she would've used it, certainly not in the workhouse where carbolic was king. I like to think she treasured it – as a keepsake – to remind her of me.

And I've planted a lavender path, in her honour. When the flowers arrive in June, I rub them between my fingers to release their oil and their scent. I close my eyes and I see her again, my Ellen, whirling around in the rainy darkness with my gift clutched in her hand.

Victorians used to say that a gift of lavender would bring luck and a promise of adventure to the receiver.

How apt that belief turned out to be.

Chapter 29

Trugs, mud and wellies

Susie
February 2019

It's Saturday morning.

My bath-time musings have proven productive again: I've come up with another idea.

Graham has popped over to have a chat with Steve, and I join them, excited to tell them about my plan. The three of us perch on the doorstep in the late winter sunshine.

I am not so excited to be telling Steve; I can predict only too accurately what his reaction will be, so I speak to Graham first. "Hey! Graham! Guess what?"

He peers at me over his glasses – he can hear my excitement.

"I've had another idea!"

"Another idea, Susie? You're full of them at the moment – whatever's got into you?" He tries to stifle a smirk.

"Stop it! I knew you'd laugh, but on the strength of my burgeoning success with the flower garden, I've been wondering about planting a vegetable patch."

"You *what?* … for Pete's sake!" It was Steve the cynic of course. He hands us our steaming mugs, gives me one of his *looks,* before raising his eyes to the sky. "You're *not*! You don't know anything about growing vegetables."

"No, I know I don't, but I know a man who does – best way to learn a new skill is to ask an expert!"

"Your good-looking, fair-haired Simon, right?" He taps his nose meaningfully, raising his eyebrows at Graham. But I'm not about to be put off by Steve's scornful attitude.

I'm quick to reply, "Absolutely: got it in one. Seriously though, if I *do* start growing vegetables, I'll be keeping up a workhouse tradition that I've read was taken up here, all those years ago."

Graham gives me a conspiratorial wink.

When I picture the type of person who grows his or her own veg or has an allotment, I have to say I'm already wondering if I'll quite fit the picture. A trug? Mud? Wellies? I'll have to give that a bit more thought. But discovering that a kitchen garden had been set up in this workhouse is inspiring, and I'm determined to give it a try.

Steve wanders off into the kitchen, with the excuse of finding more biscuits.

Graham settles down with his coffee. "Okay ... tell me all about this workhouse kitchen garden, Susie."

"I read that it even became popular in asylums."

Graham's face clouded.

"Yes, I know, *asylums* – that does sound a bit strange – but apparently patients voluntarily used their free time, the little they had, to plant and harvest vegetables. It made their plain meals more interesting, saved expense, and encouraged everyone to get some welcome fresh air."

"A bit like a large allotment."

"Yes, exactly like one. Most inmates would have grown their own fruit and veg as a matter of course before they came into the workhouse: it's what country people did in those days. Let's face it, they had little choice; it was either grow your own or go without."

We grin wryly at the thought of having to rely on home grown veg these days.

Graham asks, "And was it the workhouse for life for most of the inmates?"

"Sadly, it usually was. Once you were *in the house,* as they called it, that's where you stayed. The only way out was to find work outside or come into money. If you were no longer destitute you had no choice but to leave, but that was hardly likely to happen – as likely as winning the lottery is for us today."

Graham adds, "I don't imagine that deciding to leave would have been a difficult decision to make."

My heart sinks. I'm only too aware that the task I've set myself – helping my Ellen find *her* way out – will be an almost impossible one.

It starts to get chilly now, with a bit of a nip in the air. My cheeks are glowing but the rest of me is cold. I get up from the step.

"Okay, the sun's gone in, time to go indoors and get warmed up. Alright if I leave you two to natter in peace?"

Steve emerges from the kitchen and they wander over to the den where they can talk about Graham's computery stuff or listen to music, while I go indoors to change out of my muddy gardening clothes.

My next task is to make a list on my phone of what I might grow in my veg patch, which gives me an excuse for another enlightening visit to the garden centre to hear what my good friend Simon has to say.

Chapter 30

A posy for a pauper

Susie
February 2019

I can't keep it to myself any longer. I have to tell Steve.
Everything.

He won't be alongside me, I know he'll dismiss the whole story. He'll say what he always says: he's worried about me, I should see the doctor and tell him what I *think* I've seen and ask for some more anti-depressants. But I don't need a doctor to tell me what is becoming perfectly clear – the solution to *my* situation is emerging through untangling, or attempting to untangle, the problems of another.

I'm only too aware that the idea of experiencing two time periods won't be easy for Steve to take on board. No way. I must admit, if a friend told *me* a story like this, I would think she was making it up. I would be the one to tell her it was a crazy notion and she should get a grip.

Nevertheless, the indisputable facts are these:

When my Ellen appears, I enter her world, *one-hundred-and-thirty-eight-years ago.* I watch her, in her drab world of despair, distress and despondency; and she in turn, is able to enter *my* world of light, colour and noise. Yes, it's a pity we don't hear one another's words, but we wave and smile, and for us that is enough.

It is a unique situation but one I cherish, and it fills my mind with hope and cautious optimism, for us both.

*

We are halfway through our Friday night supper, the night

I make the effort to cook something extra special, when Steve is at home. I'm not known for my culinary skills, but tonight I've risked fillet steak with 'all the trimmings'. Kate has shown me how she cooks it, and for once I am not only surprised but delighted with the result. It should at least be a good start to Friday night.

As for the rest of the evening …

Steve is quiet as we begin our meal. Then he says, "I've been thinking."

I look up from my steak. "You've been thinking?"

He refills his glass. "Yes, I have. I think you could do with a break, get away for a bit. Leave the UK winter behind for a while. Maybe Kate would like to go with you?"

I try to put on my interested face. "Go on …" I refill my own glass.

"There're some great travel deals around at the moment, always are after Christmas. How do you fancy a week or two in the sun? I gather Cyprus is pleasantly warm at this time of year."

I guess he's hoping a holiday would provide a distraction, encourage me to 'settle down' to life as it was before the move, but that is the last thing on my mind. There is no way I'll be settling down any time soon.

I reply, "Thanks for suggesting it, and I'm sure Cyprus is beautiful, but I've got too much on. I can't go away at the moment."

I'm rewarded with his furrowed frown, lips forming a straight line, eyes closed.

I get up to fetch the warm apple pie from the oven and the cream from the fridge.

"Got room for pudding?" I wink, hoping to jolly him along. "It's your favourite."

His face remains resolute. I need to be firm about it; the best way he can help me is to let me stay right here.

Where I'm needed.

*

Gone midnight.

I wait until he's put down his book and turned off the bedside lamp. Pale moonlight streams through the sheer blue curtains.

"Steve?"

He pulls the duvet closer.

"I need to talk to you."

He keeps his back to me. "Talk to me? What about? Look, it's been a difficult week. Whatever it is, can't it wait till tomorrow? I need my sleep."

I stop myself from replying, *'And I don't need mine?'*

I put my hand on his shoulder. "I'm asking you to trust me, about the young woman I've seen in the garden. You're a sensible man: what possible reason could I have to make it up? What would be the point? I was as puzzled as you are to start with, but the more I understand what's happening, it's inspiring; and it's helping me rediscover the old me."

My moment of truth has arrived.

I inhale slowly, taking the time to pause, choosing my words carefully, "I can't ignore what's happening any longer. The truth is –"

H cuts in, "Yes, Susie, the truth is – *what?*"

I sit up, leaning against my pillow. Ready for him. "I know it's hard for you to hear, but ... I'm experiencing ... *two time periods.*"

"*Two time periods?*" He snorts into his pillow. "For goodness' sake! Did you have too much wine this evening or something? You've got to sort yourself out, this is crazy."

"Yes, I know it sounds crazy, but it's true, no question about it. I've thought long and hard but it's staring me in the face. I truly believe I'm visiting Ellen *in her time*. And she visits me in mine."

"*In her time?* You're telling me you honestly believe you travel back to the Victorian era? How does that work, for God's sake?" He plumps up his pillow to prop against the headboard and switches the bedside light back on.

I haven't the energy to go into all the details, and even if I try, I know it'll be a waste of time.

An awkward silence hangs heavily in the air, while I turn my wedding ring, unusually loose these days, on my chilled finger.

He sighs an exasperated sigh. "Look, love. You need to put these fanciful ideas of yours to bed, once and for all. Why not at least speak to Kate about going away? You'd have fun together, you know you would. You'd come home refreshed, ready to start living in the present, to stop dwelling on your imaginary workhouse world. It can't be good for you."

So, he is the expert on what's good for me all of a sudden? Where did he get that idea from?

I carry on, in my best encouraging, confident voice, "I haven't finished, Steve, I've got more to tell you. Please hear me out, you'll be glad you did."

He slumps against the pillow.

I speak gently, "I instinctively know Ellen's unhappy."

He pulls the duvet closer, and mumbles, "Of course she's unhappy if she lives in the workhouse!"

I picture his sarcastic smirk. "Stop it, Steve. Stop it, and listen to me properly for a change."

He doesn't look in my direction; in fact, I bet his eyes are shut.

"I instinctively know there's a *reason* I'm travelling to her time. It's because I'm the one who's going to help her out of her unhappiness. I am – I know it. So to make a start, I've been trying to work out a way to put her mind at rest, to reassure her."

An uneasy silence.

"Okay ... I can see her, and she can see me, but who does she think I am? And where does she think I've come from? What does she imagine is happening to her when she finds herself in our garden and not in the workhouse yard?"

He tenses up his whole body.

"So, I worked out that the best way to show her I'm real and not to be feared, was to leave her a gift. Something that couldn't have come from the workhouse."

Another loud, exasperated sigh from Steve.

I refuse to be daunted. "I decided to choose something luxurious, something she won't be used to. I left her my bar of lavender scented soap. I put it on the step near the long grass where she's been feeding Mittens. And it's gone. I watched her discover it."

"*What?* You're telling me you actually saw her find it?" He turns his back and starts to pummel his pillow again.

I'm on a roll. "Yes, I really did. I wish you'd been there to see it. She was thrilled to bits."

He huffs and puffs but there's no going back for me now.

"And our garden," I almost lose my nerve and grip the edge of the duvet with both hands. "Our garden – became – the *workhouse yard*!"

The bed shakes as his shoulders slump.

"It was in near total darkness, only a few candles at bare windows. No lawn, no plants, no holly tree, only the bare workhouse yard!"

Telling him these details makes me feel I've grown up at last. I'm finally facing life in a realistic way, emerging from the restriction of my self-imposed chrysalis. And, to my delight, I'm loving it.

I gather pace. "And not only did I see her find the soap but I'm certain she knew it was a gift from me."

"Oh, *Susie* …" Steve speaks more calmly. "You're in a bad way, love. You must see this is not normal behaviour – talking about travelling in time, believing you can help her. She lived here well over a hundred years ago, for God's sake. I'm sorry love, but none of this works for me."

He switches off the lamp again.

I can't see his hands in the dark, but instinct tells me he's clenching his fists.

I've got this far; I'm not going to stop now. "We waved at one another through the window. It's obvious she can see me as easily as I can see her. We both had tears in our eyes."

A loud groan from Steve. "And what are you going to leave for her next? *A box of tissues for her tears?*"

I plough on, "What I need to focus on at the moment is communicating with her; to show her I'm here, sharing her workhouse world, trying to help her. I don't yet know how I'm going to do it but I know I can and I will, once she gains confidence and learns to trust me. That's what inspired me to leave her the soap."

He grabs the bottle of water from his bedside table and indulges in several loud gulps. In his best unsympathetic tone he adds, "Have you finished? Or is there more?"

I decide to go for it. After all, what have I got to lose?

"I'm going to follow this up, Steve, to build her trust. I've been thinking about what else would please her, what she would love, and wouldn't have access to in the workhouse."

A disheartening – but not unexpected – silence.

I speak carefully. "So – I'm going to leave her some flowers."

Steve almost chokes on his water. "Of course you are. I hear *Interflora* was gaining popularity in the eighteen-hundreds."

"Stop it! You're not being fair. I've given this a lot of thought. I'm going to pick her a bunch of snowdrops; the churchyard is still full of them. She can't get out to pick them herself, so I'll do it for her. I'll tie them into a posy. She'll love them, I know she will. But I'd like you to do one important thing for me."

He downs more water, like a parched traveller struggling in the desert.

"I'd like you to wait with me to watch her find the snowdrops. Once you've seen her for yourself, you'll understand how I feel, and we can move on. We could help her together."

I screw up my eyes. His next words will be crucial. I wish he could understand how much our future rests on his next reaction.

He turns around to face me. "Okay, if it will put a stop to all this nonsense, once and for all, I'll watch with you this time. But when there's nothing to see, and we both know there won't be," I cross my fingers and hold my breath, "you'll have to accept that I'll have nothing more to do with this whole ridiculous scenario. You can go back to talk to the doctor about it, get some more medication and we'll live our normal lives again, put it all behind us."

There's nothing more I can say.

"Now. Can I please be allowed to get some sleep?"

He turns over, drags most of the duvet to his side and is soon snoring, while I lie perfectly still, wide awake, struggling to prevent my anxious tears from flowing.

*

And so it is the next day I stroll around our churchyard, admiring the amazing carpet of nodding snowdrops. No, I know I shouldn't be picking them, but I don't feel guilty – and I only pick a few. It's such a good cause.

I tell myself God won't mind; in fact, he'll be delighted to provide a posy for a pauper.

Chapter 31

Dancing for joy – again

Ellen
February 1881

Jane walks straight past it, seeing nothing out of place. But it's there, on the edge of the doorstep. How can she have missed it?

James and the girls look pale and worn out. They stumble up the pitch-black stairs, guided by Jane carrying our candle. It's her turn to get the children ready for bed.

I open the door to check the step once more, in case I was mistaken, but there it is, a tiny posy of delicate snowdrops, tied together with a piece of straw.

For me.

My benefactor has left me a second gift. And why would that be? I'm confident now of the answer – because she wants me to trust her, as a friend.

I'm spellbound.

I gather up the flowers and held them to my nose, closing my eyes to breathe in their delicate fragrance. Then, without stopping to think about it, I start to dance, all over again. Round and round the rain swept yard I whirl, faster and faster, my woollen dress swirling and twirling in the damp night air. Feelings I never thought to feel in the house – vibrancy, vivaciousness and vitality – flow through me.

I'm dancing ... for joy.

Because I'm *free*.

Yes, I'm in the house, but for these precious moments, I'm *free*. As I dance, a misty moon makes its way out from behind the clouds to light up the path, and my fears are swept away, like dead leaves in an autumn breeze.

A weight has been lifted; my world is about to change. My benefactor has travelled from her world of light, colour and strange sounds, to support me in my life of gloom, bleak surroundings and quietness, and somehow, she will help me leave it all behind.

*

Summer 1911

I loved my posy.

I placed it in our parlour, in a teacup, and it lasted for several glorious days on the mantelshelf. Neither Jane nor Matron mentioned it.

And why was that?

Because it was intended for my eyes, and my eyes alone.

Discovering those precious gifts marked the establishment of an otherworldly time for me. Day by day, my faith grew, in what some would dismiss as the demented delusions of a destitute workhouse pauper, in grave danger of swift admittance to the asylum.

Have you ever been so happy that you danced? It's a unique feeling and one I haven't experienced often in my life. On that memorable night, I danced for joy, for friendship and for freedom.

Chapter 32

Only a misty moon …

Susie
February 2019

I cross my fingers as we wait together in the kitchen with the light off. Only the porch lamp shines a path across the wet lawn. It would be comforting if Steve made an effort and held my hand, despite his reluctance to be here, but it's obvious he only longs for it to be over. No room for loving gestures.

Evening is the time I look out for her, when her supper is finished. Our broken clock is making itself heard, and as it nears seven o'clock the light outside starts to fade, as I knew it would, and the garden dissolves into the bleak, wet yard. No porch light now, only a few stubby tallow candles flickering at curtainless windows.

Surely Steve can hear the loud ticking? Doesn't he wonder where the sound is coming from?

Ellen drifts towards the cottage, her shawl wrapped around her against the rain, ready to feed Mittens, at the same time keeping an eye out for any inmate who might disturb her on their way back from supper.

Before crouching down to leave the food amongst the wet grass, she pauses, frowning, and stares at the step where the tiny posy waits, sprinkled with raindrops. She looks up at this kitchen window, shyly smiles at me, and waves.

She bites her bottom lip and puts her a hand up to her mouth as she stares at the posy. She risks another quick glance behind her, before she tenderly gathers up the delicate flowers and lifts them to her nose – as she did with the soap.

Her slim body begins to sway in the darkness of the yard, whirling faster and faster, and she randomly touches her wan face with the rain refreshed snowdrops as she dances.

I can hardly breathe as I watch her, witnessing something as precious as this: *my Ellen is dancing for joy in the rain, with only a misty moon for company.*

I'm totally caught up in the moment, desperate to know if Steve is sharing it. I squeeze his arm and look up at his face, my eyes alert. I press my nails into my palms. Is this when it will all come crashing down?

His cheeks twitch before he sucks in his lips and turns away, not bothering to look at me.

"That's it, Susie. I've done what you asked. I've waited with you to see your *friend* discover the posy. I've dutifully stood here for the last fifteen minutes, looking out of our kitchen window and, guess what? I'm seeing exactly what I see every evening – our garden, lawn, flower borders, holly tree and Joan's birdbath. Now there's a surprise!"

I hate his tone.

My hands are stinging.

So is my heart.

He spits out the words, "Yes, the snowdrops have gone – blown away in the wind I expect – but there's been no one else in our garden tonight, only Mittens. End of."

I watch, defeated, as he slams the kitchen door behind him and escapes over to his den. I stumble upstairs, throw myself on our bed, and sob.

*

Watching Ellen dance for joy in the misty moonlight was a pivotal moment for me. I've never seen anything like it since and no doubt never will again.

She danced as if she hadn't a care in her world, and as I watched her, my emerging self told me the time had come to stop lying to myself, to stop expecting him to change. Steve is a lost cause.

It's time to stop listening to his put-downs and snide remarks.

It's time to leave him to it.

And it's time – for *me* to dance – to my own tune.

Chapter 33

Beyond the house

Ellen
March 1881

It's the recreation hour, a perfect opportunity to speak to Jane. I feel at ease discussing things with her, she always listens to my ideas and is never quick to judge.

I sit down by the fire. "I have an idea I'd like to share with you, Jane. Can you spare me a moment?"

She gives me one of her knowing looks, as I start to explain, "I've been thinking about our future, beyond the house."

A wry smile appears on her careworn face. "I wish I believed there could be a better future waiting for me and my girls. All I can picture ahead for us is distressing despair and drudgery."

The fire is doing its best to chase away the winter chill that creeps insidiously into every nook and cranny of the cottage, and our minds.

I go on, "There are only two ways we can leave here – one is to find employment outside, and the other is to come into money. The prospect of staying here until I die fills me with horror as I'm sure it does you. Our children deserve the chance to learn a trade, perhaps get taken on as apprentices, to provide a living for a family of their own one day. There's a limit to what the house can do to prepare any of our young inmates in that regard."

Jane nods.

"I'm convinced that those long years of hard work alongside Father as his gardener's boy deserve to bear fruit. Before Joe comes home and we can go back to live with Mother, I've decided to get myself ready to seek a position on the Longmead estate, working for the new head gardener. It would mean another wage coming in and combined with Mother's laundry work and Joe's money, we'd be able to manage."

We reach out our hands as the fire springs to life.

"I've devised a perfect plan to resolve two problems at once – I can sharpen up my gardening skills ready for possible future employment and, at the same time, extend our meagre fare here in the house."

She turns to face me, her face expectant, as I continue, "I'm planning to ask the Master and Matron to let us create a kitchen garden, for the benefit of the house. There's plenty of room in the rough ground at the end of the yard. The older boys and young men would profit from learning a useful set of skills that would come in handy if they ever have the chance to leave, and the pantry shelves would soon be filled with our own home grown produce. Everyone would benefit."

Jane draws down her lips. "I'm not sure they'll allow it, Ellen. We're worked off our feet already, what with the never-ending laundry, constant cleaning and cooking tasks. A kitchen garden would take a lot of keeping up. How would we find the time?"

I'm anxious to have her on my side. "Don't worry, Jane, I've thought about that. After our day's work is finished, and we've had our supper, we could use the recreation hour. Neither Master nor Matron could object to some of us doing an hour's gardening work in our own time, could they?"

Jane raises her eyebrows.

"Once spring is here and the light returns, we'll relish working in the open air, and on Sunday afternoons it will give us something purposeful to do. As soon as they see the advantages of producing some of our own food, and how well the guardians will receive such a thrifty plan, I'm confident they will give their approval."

Jane gives me one of her special smiles. "I have every faith – if anyone can persuade them, you're the one to do it."

We share a hug before reluctantly leaving our seats by the fire, to put the children to bed.

All I need to do now, is put my idea forward … and wait.

Chapter 34

Only a woman

Ellen
March 1881

There is someone important I would like to discuss my plan with before approaching Matron. Sarah, one of our oldest inmates.

The house has been her home for many a year. She is a loving, motherly person and I can count on her to advise me wisely, so I've made time to visit her after supper.

She loves to tell us tales of her younger married days; helping with the allotment, growing vegetables, and rearing the family pig before her husband died, when, like us, she had no choice but to take the house.

Sarah's cottage is a perfect snuggery with nothing out of place. I peep through her bare but shining window and there she is, in her long grey woollen gown and blue shawl, a clean white smock and her bonnet. She's busy with a pile of mending.

I tap on her door, she calls out a friendly greeting and I lift the latch. "I trust I'm not disturbing you, Sarah?"

She's sitting close to her fire, enjoying the benefit of its warmth and light for her sewing, saving her precious candle.

She smiles, her sweet face bearing few signs of age. "Ellen my dear, it does me a power of good to see you. Your cheery manner never fails to gladden my heart."

"How are you tonight? I see you're at your sewing, as usual."

"I'm doing as well as ever – thank you for asking – despite the problems that old age brings. Come and sit with me by the fire."

She offers me her choicest seat, made extra comfortable with one of her patchwork cushions. We stretch out our hands to the welcome warmth.

"I've come to ask your opinion on an important matter."

She puts down her spectacles and sets her sewing aside.

"I've been making plans for our future life, when my Joe comes home, and we can afford to live back with Mother again."

She inclines her head and gives me a quizzical glance.

"It's like this. I'm considering asking the Master and Matron for permission to create a kitchen garden for the benefit of us all."

She waits for me to explain.

"We could make good use of the rough ground in front of the far wall, near the privies. Growing our own vegetables would provide extra food for the house and any surplus could be sold off at the market for a well-deserved profit. I'm seeking counsel from our older and more experienced inmates and I'm wondering, how does the idea strike you?"

She places the stocking she was darning on the arm of her chair, while a droll smile forms on her fire-warmed cheeks. "You're a dark horse, and no mistake, Ellen. As if you haven't got enough to do …"

I grin cheekily.

"When are you considering approaching the Master?"

"I shall speak to him in due course, but I'm keen to have your opinion beforehand. What do you think? Am I being too bold? Will the Master and Matron dismiss me as merely an inmate and *only a woman* at that?"

Sarah stretches forward in her chair and uses the poker to enliven the struggling fire. "You were very fortunate to be taken on as your father's gardener's boy, weren't you, Ellen? Did his other gardeners poke fun at a young *woman* taking on such a role, and pour scorn on your efforts?"

I smile at the memories. "Yes, they did to start with, but Father soon put a stop to it and forbade them to treat me as their inferior. With his guidance I was quick to learn the job and they soon came to respect me, once they saw I could carry out my duties to the same high standard as they did. They wouldn't have risked getting into Father's bad books in case he told the squire and they lost their jobs."

Sarah chuckles. "Women should be free to be as bold as any man, my dear, although I know it's not fashionable to say so. And," she pauses shyly, "they should receive the same pay as the men, for doing the same work."

"I agree, and how I wish more women would voice that opinion. But many are ruled by fear and accept they only deserve to take on lowly positions, as maids of all work, for little reward." We fall silent, deep in thought, not daring to believe that circumstances will ever alter in that regard.

The fire crackles, interrupting our musings. Sarah moves closer to its warmth, rubbing her hands as she gives me one of her serious looks, keen to get down to the purpose of my visit.

"You know it'll be the guardians who'll have the final say about your idea. They have charge of every expense for the house."

I reply, "Indeed they will, and they'll have to be consulted of course, but if money can be saved on the purchase of vegetables and fruit, and the work is carried out by our able-bodied inmates, they cannot raise any great objection, can they?"

Sarah strokes her chin. "The Master is the person who'll put your plan in front of the guardians. He'll expect you to explain the details to him, as he'll be the one to oversee the work, if it is agreed. But it's a good idea to speak to Matron first; we know how much the Master respects her views."

I nod my agreement. In truth, we all know it is Matron who organises the house, despite what she likes to tell us to the contrary.

"Arthur Bates is another useful person you might talk

to, next time you're scrubbing floors over on the men's side. I understand he was employed as a garden labourer before he took the house, as were several of the retired men. They'll have the skills and experience you're looking for and will enjoy showing the young ones what to do. If we could encourage them to join in with some of the less arduous tasks, it would make a welcome change, much better than sitting around idle when their day's work is done."

I nod again. Idleness is a condition rarely experienced or even spoken of in the house.

"I agree, Sarah. The children will love to get involved and it would be an ideal chance for them to be outdoors. They could help with weeding and carrying water from the well in the lane to our water butt. We'll use considerable amounts of water."

Now we are both grinning broadly; it looks as if my plan could well become a reality. I can tell Sarah has faith in me where others in the house might dismiss my plan.

She stands up. "I think it's time for a cup of tea to celebrate your brave idea." She potters over to the dresser where, as an older inmate, she's allowed to keep her own blue and white china teapot and a caddy for her daily tea ration. "Nothing like a good brew to warm us up on a winter's night."

After our welcome drinks, I say, "I'll come over to tell you what Matron has to say, Sarah. Let's hope it'll be good news."

Her advice is sensible, as I'd known it would be. I will put my idea to Matron, one morning, while we peel the potatoes for our dinners. If all goes to plan, we could be producing our own crops by the summer, and I'll have taken an important step towards my possible future employment.

As I hasten back along the yard, I'm met by the unexpected but welcome sight of my colourful stranger, in her red coat, standing at the open door of our cottage. I lift a hand to shield my eyes, as the brightest of lamplight streams across the yard. Once again it has transformed into a garden and the chill wind is causing the pretty blue curtains at her upstairs window to blow about.

From somewhere inside, a clock is ticking – loudly – while she smiles warmly at me. We gaze at one another across the grass until her image fades, along with the colours, and I am left alone once more, in the grey, grim, silence of the workhouse yard.

Except – *I'm not alone, am I?*

My red-coated stranger is here. Every day my trust in her grows stronger, but I have as yet no understanding of what kind of help she might be able to give me.

The evening takes on a warm atmosphere, despite the cold, and not only because a lamp had been shining radiantly on our cottage wall.

Chapter 35

The proposition

Ellen
March 1881

I can't wait any longer; it's time to screw up my courage to approach Matron. She isn't such a bad old stick if you catch her in an amiable frame of mind. She does her best for us, with limited funds, and a kind heart hides beneath her sometimes-harsh exterior.

I bide my time until my morning's scrubbing and kitchen work is finished. She's taking a few precious minutes to sit down with a cup of tea, before it's time to dish up our dinners.

I stand as tall as I can, pulling my shoulders back and wearing my friendliest smile.

"Excuse me, Matron? May I trouble you for a moment please?"

She raises an eyebrow, sipping her tea.

"I would like to ask for your support, Matron."

She lets out a sigh and a frown appears. "Support, Ellen? What can you possibly want with my support?" She pulls in her thin lips. "There's plenty of work waiting to be done today so don't think you're going to shirk it, wasting your time gossiping to me, my girl."

I instinctively turn my wedding ring, trying to ward off my nerves. I speak bravely, "I hope you know I'm not one to waste my time, Matron, and I would certainly never waste yours."

I close my eyes for a moment. Will she take kindly to my suggestion or will she dismiss the idea out of hand? My face is flushed, and not simply from the hot water I'd used for my morning's floor scrubbing.

I take a deep breath and say it plainly. "I have a proposition I hope you will consider, Matron."

I pause to gather my strength before continuing; my mouth has gone dry. "I would like to ask you and the Master to consider giving your permission for some of us to establish a kitchen garden, here in the yard, for the benefit of the house."

At last.

My plan is out in the open.

She stops, with her cup halfway to her mouth. I have her undivided attention.

"With the Master's permission, Matron, my idea is for us inmates to make use of the patch of rough grass by the wall at the far end of the yard. It's the perfect place for a kitchen garden; there's plenty of room to grow vegetables, and the produce would be of considerable benefit to everyone."

Matron puts down her cup. "You want to grow vegetables? For the house? Well I'm blowed! I don't know what comes over you, young lady. Aren't we keeping you busy enough? What will you come up with next?"

I will have to summon all my guile to persuade her to put my idea with the Master; she likes him to believe all innovations have come from him. We know different of course.

I've heard it said that Matron has a fine reputation with the guardians for being thrifty. A money-saving idea like mine will surely meet with her approval, and more importantly, with theirs.

I play my winning card. "If we could grow our own vegetables, Matron, it would go down very well with the guardians. I know it costs the rate-payers dearly to keep us fed."

She gets up abruptly, tipping away the tea she'd let go cold, quickly washing the cup and saucer in the stone sink. She wipes her hands on her apron, and speaks briskly, "I think you've wasted enough of my time for one day, my girl. Get back to work now, instead of filling your head with grand schemes you should leave to your elders and betters."

She ushers me firmly out of the kitchen, but I am not deterred. I am well aware she will *not* forgo an opportunity to win the praise of the guardians. In the meantime, the worst thing I can do is try to prolong the conversation.

And the best thing I can do is wait.

Chapter 36

A wobble

Susie
March 2019

It's not easy to accept that your once loving husband has changed, that he's never going to be on your side again. Steve is so determined to disprove my story, so relentless with his criticism, that I've allowed serious doubts to mount up.

And not only about what I've been seeing.

After the euphoria of deciding to embrace what life could hold for me, and bravely making my plans, I can't ignore it; I'm having a major wobble. Perhaps it's time to abandon the whole project, to forget about Ellen and the workhouse, everything I've read online, and put the whole experience down to my unstable mental state. Should I go back to the *sensibl*e route and settle for the empty life I led before we moved?

The fact that Steve will never share my acceptance of the presence of Ellen, and constantly pricks my fragile balloon of belief, has seriously dented my confidence. I feel isolated, stuck in what Steve would call my fantasy world. It's time to make some important decisions.

Am I fooling myself in trying to help Ellen?

Could it be that Steve is right when he says it's simply that I want it to be true, therefore it is?

Am I subconsciously using this whole situation as a displacement activity?

I have to admit I can see where he's coming from. The facts are these:

He doesn't see her.

He hasn't watched her feeding and fussing Mittens.

He isn't seeing or hearing anything out of the ordinary. *Nothing at all.*

But the undeniable fact remains – *I am.*

On the other hand, my sensitive, creative side assures me that I'm *not* losing the plot. Yes, of course I'll be overjoyed if everything I've been experiencing is real, but at the same time, I can understand a *small* amount of Steve's negative attitude. He has no evidence for any of it except what I've told him. He genuinely believes I've lost it.

A bit of a vicious circle, to say the least.

Sometimes, when I'm feeling particularly low, I console myself by accepting that my recent time travelling experiences would be too much to expect *any* rational person to take on board. I need an objective view on all this, and I know I can rely on Kate and Graham to give me an unbiased, balanced opinion; they'll be honest and fair. They've tried their best to help me face up to my marriage issues over the years, and to cope with our loss.

I decide to give them a ring while I'm in an open frame of mind. They're happy to help and I'm soon driving over to see them. Talking it through with old friends is the best way to dig myself out of this dark hole.

Unsurprisingly, I start to feel better the moment Kate opens the door. I give them both a hug and they encourage me to make myself comfortable on their squashy sofa.

"What's all this about, Susie? You sounded a bit harassed on the phone. Something the matter?"

Kate has an uncanny knack of picking up on emotions in my telephone voice; I call her my friendly witch.

She starts the ball rolling. "I'm glad you've come over, Susie. I've been worried about you – you're not yourself these days. We both saw how lost you were before the move, how you were drifting through your days, depressed, *putting up* with life. Such a waste. Life is for living, living with zest. We hated to see you like that, and now it sounds as if you're battling with Steve all over again."

Too true. And I like her choice of the word 'battling'. That's exactly what I'm doing.

She's quite right – before the move, I'd been drifting. But the cottage and everything it stands for has been trying to show me it *is* possible to find the old me.

The last thing I need right now, is this *wobble*.

*

It's a relief to share my misgivings, and once I've gathered my thoughts, I'm ready to explain.

"I'm very lucky to have you two to listen. Sometimes I go round and round in circles, wondering whether what Steve says is true and my imagination *is* playing tricks. It's this whole issue of Ellen and the workhouse; it's getting me down. I worry believing that I travel to her time, and she travels to mine is all in my mind; not real."

They both smile warmly. Kate offers me a piece of her homemade shortbread and we get ready to enjoy a welcome pot of coffee.

She is her typical empathetic self. "I know it's hard. After everything that's happened it's natural you should be looking for a new path until you're ready to go back to teaching."

I lean forward, resting my hands on my knees. "The thing is, Steve has sorted out *his* role. He spends more and more hours at his consultancy work, often until late into the night. He never talks about the miscarriage and he never encourages me to. It's his way. He chooses *not* to deal with it. The result is, he's allowed the wedge between us to grow. He's never going to change his attitude. I have to accept that I've got to do this on my own."

Graham smiles a comforting smile. "You're not on your own, Susie; you know we're always here for you."

I finger the tissue in my pocket as I go on. "I'd hoped Steve would be pleased I'd found a project, one that focused on someone else's misery rather than my own. Surely that must be a good thing? But he absolutely refuses to support me, in fact he doesn't miss a chance to poke fun. He has neither the inclination or ability to cave in and let go of his expectation to always be right."

Kate sighs quietly.

"I want to be angry with him. I want him to see himself as I see him nowadays – selfish, thoughtless and insensitive. What happened, happened to us both. Sadly, his way of dealing with it is to bluster on about unrelated stuff and never talk about it; that way he can tell himself he has no obligation to be involved."

They share sad glances.

"He's incapable of seeing things as I do. Yes, he used to, but not anymore. Why doesn't he at least take an interest in what I'm telling him? Why would I be making this up? What possible reason could I have for doing that?" I fight back against my hot, angry tears. "My only conclusion has to be this: Ellen and I aren't the only ones living in two completely different worlds."

Kate moves a bit closer to put a gentle hand on my arm. "It's such a shame. The point is, he doesn't realise this whole episode could be the answer for you. Graham and I feel that working on this new project will really help you. You mustn't give up on it. Not yet anyway."

My voice wavers. "The trouble is, I've been meandering around in the mist of misery for such a long time. Steve copes by working too hard and pretending everything's okay. But it's not, is it?" I can't help it. I blink frantically at my two trusted friends as I lose the battle with my tears and grab hold of the tissue.

Kate's voice is soothing. "The point is, he doesn't like it that you see Ellen and he doesn't; he feels left out. It could be he's convinced himself this is all the result of your grief, and that your mind has conjured up the whole workhouse scenario because you're desperately searching for a replacement. Someone to look after."

I look down at the floor and fiddle with my wedding ring.

Kate puts her arm around my shoulders. "We know he doesn't see things as you do, but he should try to be kinder about it. More tolerant. I think it would be better if you treat this as solely your project and let him get on with his life. It's the only way." Kate is valiantly trying to see both sides. "You're only making yourself more upset by hoping he's going to change. And he isn't, I'm afraid."

I wipe my cheeks and accept another piece of comforting shortbread. "I've been wanting to talk to both of you about it, for ages. As our oldest friends, you'll tell me the truth and not simply pretend to support me, just to make me feel better."

I lean back against the soft patchwork cushions, feeling myself relax. "Right, you two; now it's time to give me a dose of your wisdom about the whole wider scenario."

Kate raises her eyebrows, looks over at Graham, and they both pretend to be suitably flattered at my use of the word 'wisdom'.

"I want you to be straight with me."

Simply knowing that Kate and Graham are there and ready to listen, however foolish my story might appear, makes all the difference. They put down their coffee mugs.

"Here's the thing. I really need to ask you this: do you accept that it's possible to see – okay, let's call it what it is – a *ghost?* Have either of you ever seen one?"

Kate gives me a reassuring smile. "No, I haven't, but Graham reckons he has, don't you, love?" She catches hold of my hand, knowing how important this is to me.

Graham peers genially over his spectacles. "Yes, as a matter of fact I do."

My eyes don't leave his face.

He begins, "I was driving home from work one night in early winter, a few years back …"

I can't wait to hear this.

"I was passing the river when I saw him."

Goosebumps.

"You *saw* him?"

Graham speaks softly, "Well, I know it was nearly dark and some might say I was imagining it, but I'm sure I saw a young lad wandering about at the edge of the road, close to the river. He had a look of the early 1940s about him. He was wearing a tweed jacket that was far too big, a cloth cap, short trousers and knee-high socks, and he was crying bitterly."

I put down my coffee. "What did you do?"

"Well, I parked the car and waited at the roadside for a few minutes, watching through the window. We all know you have to be careful about approaching any child these days, particularly when it's nearly dark, and I admit I did dither a bit. But this is the worst part: before I had a chance to speak to him, he didn't hesitate, he walked straight into the fast-flowing river. And that was the last I saw of him."

I bite my lip. Hard. "Oh, my goodness …"

"I phoned the police and they carried out a full search, but he was never found."

We sit quietly, trying to picture the scene.

Eventually I ask, "Are you confident you saw the *ghost* of that poor boy?"

"Difficult question. No, I can't know for absolute certainty, but I am reasonably confident. I do believe it's possible for some of us to see things we don't necessarily understand."

I turn to Kate. "What do you think, Kate? Are you with Graham on this?"

She frowns slightly. "Well, I wasn't there to see it, but yes, I do think it's possible. And even more importantly, I think that you *are* seeing Ellen, and, that you're seeing her *in her time as well as in ours*."

My shoulders relax on hearing their words and my heartbeat slows down a little. I give them each an enormous hug; it feels as if I've had a reprieve.

So it's true. I'm not living in a fantasy world. My experiences with Ellen are *real,* just as my instincts have told me.

On my drive home, passing the same river, I think about that tragic child, and I agree with what Graham said: that some of us are privileged to see and hear things that may never be explained.

Chapter 37

The Master

Ellen
March 1881

I've only had to wait for two days to be summoned to speak to the Master in the office, a few minutes before dinnertime.

I hurry to put on a fresh apron and tidy my hair in the cracked looking glass as best I can, before knocking cautiously on the weighty wooden door. He calls out "Come in," in a bold voice, but a voice that commands respect rather than fear.

I stand in front of the imposing black leather-topped desk, strewn with thick ledgers, pens and smudged ink pots; and of course, with the special clock overseeing all proceedings. He settles his thin frame in the high-backed chair and gives me a knowing smile.

"Well, Ellen. It has come to my notice that you've been conjuring up an ambitious plan."

I try hard not to show my nervousness, keeping a confident smile on my face.

"Matron has informed me of your scheme to create a kitchen garden for the benefit of the house. She tells me you're of the opinion that it could help produce more varied food, save us some expense, and at the same time, provide useful work for our more mobile inmates."

I listen attentively, trying not to raise my hopes too high.

"Well, Ellen. I must say you never cease to amaze me."

I can't help but blush.

"And I'm sure you'll be pleased to hear that this is a suggestion of which I wholeheartedly approve."

I realise I've been holding my breath. I let it out quietly.

He goes on, "In my previous position as assistant at the county asylum, we encouraged our more able-bodied patients to establish a large area specially for vegetables. I hope you won't think me boastful, but it proved most productive, and more important, profitable."

This is far more than I could've hoped for.

"However, I have to ask you – because the guardians will need to know – do you possess the necessary skills and knowledge to carry out such work? And do we have sufficient inmates able to help? Or will we simply be squandering parishioners' money?"

I take a step closer to his desk. "Yes, Master, I do have the skills; my father taught me well. He had a well-paid role as head gardener at Longmead House over in Bishopstoke, and I was employed as his gardener's boy from the age of fourteen, for six years."

I can see he is somewhat taken aback at the notion of a young woman taking on a role normally carried out by a young man; not a situation he is used to.

He fingers his whiskery chin, deep in thought, before continuing. "Well, Ellen. I will have to work out the costs of tools and seeds and draw up some strict rules before I can consider putting the plan in front of the guardians, but all being well I shall consult them at next week's meeting. As you know, they have to keep a watchful eye on the accounts, so I cannot make any promises about how they'll receive the idea."

I just manage to stop myself from jumping up and down with excitement. "Oh Master, thank you! Thank you for listening to me and not dismissing my idea out of hand."

He gets up. "I'm always ready to listen, Ellen; it costs nothing, but I hope it's valuable."

I want to give him a hug for his kindness. I decide to take a chance, while he's in this frame of mind, and mention my plan for possible future employment.

"There's something else I'd like your help with, Master, if you can spare me a few more minutes."

He looks up at the clock. "Just a few then, Ellen; it'll soon be time for you to go back to the kitchen."

I put on my best smile. "It's like this, Master ..." I take a breath. "I'm thinking about asking our squire if I could work on his estate again, once my husband has found fresh work and we can leave the house. With my wages to add to his and Mother's we'd be able to manage fairly well."

He fingers his chin.

"I'm sure that starting a kitchen garden here would help prepare me to take on such work again."

I look at his face and cross my fingers behind my back ...

And I'm not disappointed.

He stands up. "Well, Ellen, you're certainly full of interesting ideas this morning. I think the squire would be lucky to have you work for him again. We'll have to see what we can do to help."

I can't hide my excitement; my face says it all.

"But now it's time for you to get back to the kitchen. Matron will be wondering what's keeping you so long. I'll let you know how the guardians receive your idea, in due course."

The twelve o'clock dinner bell and the clock's chime put an end to our conversation.

It's hard to be patient when you're young; to wait, to do nothing, to say nothing. Patience has never been part of my character, but it can serve you well.

for her, allowing Jane and the children to walk ahead. My customary tasty titbits are ready in my apron pocket and yes – here she is – trotting towards me, tail high in the air, her pristine paws showing up clearly in the evening's gloom.

I shield my eyes with my hand in delight as the yard puts on its now familiar show; the extraordinary but glorious lamps are lit and colour arrives to replace the workhouse drabness. Paws bounces across the garden to rub against my legs as I bend to leave her my scraps. I listen to her purr her greeting, for my ears alone.

I'm blessed to have her befriend me, and not only because she relies on me for her food. She is my trusted ally; she will never judge or mock. She listens without interrupting, soothing my troubled mind, giving me the space to gather my thoughts.

She lifts me out of my distress, allowing me to see beyond our hopelessness, towards a better life that, until recent days, has seemed out of reach. She is an envoy from this rare world I've been chosen to enter.

Paws is unique among cats.

And why is that?

Because she's able to travel in time.

I look up at the brightly lit window, and yes; my trusted friend is there, looking out for me, smiling and waving. I cling to the notion that she's come to me for a very special reason, yet to be revealed.

Later, lying awake, my body aching with cold, frosty stars glittering outside our window, I indulge myself in believing that our lives will change. I have every faith in both my colourful stranger and my little cat to help me find the key to our freedom.

I hug myself tightly under the thin blanket, while a growing awareness that the impossible might be possible steadily seeps into my mind: that one day we *will* leave the house. We are not destined to remain paupers, tainted for the rest of our lives. If I can hold on to my faith and courage, things will change. Joe will be coming home with

Chapter 38

Even a pauper

Ellen
August 1911

Do you have a pet?

If you do, don't underestimate its power to enhance your life in immeasurable ways. My life today would be incomplete without Paws, she never ceases to amaze me. She trots ahead of me in the garden, as she used to in the house, sniffing about for treats and keeping the mice and voles at bay.

And how she loves it by the fire. Curls up on her favourite old wooden chair, to spend the night on her special patchwork cushion.

Everyone loves her. My neighbours' children pop over to leave scraps of food for her in the patch of long grass by our kitchen door, as I used to do, all those years ago.

They often ask me how long I've had her, but if I told them the truth, they'd only laugh.

Sometimes she disappears for a while, but always comes home when she's hungry. I don't worry about her – I know exactly where she goes ...

*

Ellen
March 1881

I hope I won't be disappointed. With a bit of luck my Paws will be loitering in the darkness, waiting for me.

As we traipse back across the darkening yard, after our bread, cheese and small beer supper, I hang back to look good news.

But later, as I continue to shiver in the gloom, I look around the bare, bleak bedroom and give myself a stiff talking to in my head – I tell myself to face up to reality.

Leave the house?

Every pauper knows there is but one way out of the house before your death: you must prove you have *money*.

And not a pittance either.

In the chill darkness surrounding me, I struggle to sweep away my negative thoughts.

After all's said and done, we are all entitled to have a dream.

Even a pauper.

Chapter 39

"You can't eat flowers."

Ellen
March 1881

After the excitement of putting my plans before the Master and Matron, I decide to risk suggesting we could grow flowers as well as vegetables. I don't expect Matron to receive the idea with enthusiasm; in fact, I'm prepared for a bit of a battle to get her to agree.

I'm eager to tell Mother all about my plans at her next visit. I make sure I give due acknowledgement to Matron for her initial cautious support for the whole kitchen garden idea. I am well aware she has left the office door ajar, to eavesdrop, as is her habit.

I'm anxious to begin. "At last, Mother, at last I can see a new life ahead for our family. Once Joe is settled in his new job, I'm going to seek a garden labourer's position on the Longmead estate. I know my wages won't be high, but with mine and Joe's wages coming in and your laundry money, we'll be able to manage as a family once more, so long as we're frugal."

Mother is beaming. "Your dear father would be thankful your long apprenticeship with him wasn't wasted, love. You can't fail to impress the squire with an application to work for him again, I have complete confidence in you."

She can tell I am serious about taking up my gardening work for the squire. Gardening has always been my strength, as it is today. I've always known that Mother is proud of me, but it feels good to be reassured.

She asks, "What are you intending to grow in this kitchen garden? Are you planning to produce solely vegetables?"

I sense Matron's ears will be pricking up. "Well, Mother, I am hoping Matron might allow us to include some flowers; wild ones like bluebells, forget-me-nots and primroses, to start with. A bunch of flowers would cheer the office, as well as bringing life and colour to our parlours."

Mother's face shows her approval.

"I've also been wondering about asking the Master if he will allow some of the men to build a simple wooden bench in the yard, where our less able-bodied inmates could sit to take the air on warm days. It would do them good to rest in a yard with some flowers to cheer them."

Matron interrupts us as she comes back into the office. "I don't know where Ellen got this silly idea from, Mrs Freeborn. We can't throw parishioners' precious money away on *flowers*. I have made it perfectly clear: *you can't eat flowers.* That's that – and all there is to it."

Mother hugs me close when it's time to say goodbye and whispers "I think we'll have to see about that, don't you?"

I'm itching to discover what her words might imply, although I could hazard a guess, but I don't wish to risk Matron's displeasure by saying any more to Mother on the topic, in her hearing.

I walk with Mother to the gates to wave her off, but this time neither of us feels so despondent. She's always been one to enjoy a secret and I can see she's in her element with this one. She'll not let Matron have the final word, if she can do something about it.

I can't help smile at the mischievous grin on her face when she turns around in the lane to wave goodbye, before hurrying on her way.

*

I'm bursting with excitement.

Mother is here again, a few days later, as I knew she would be, bringing us a substantial parcel. Thankfully

Matron merely gives the contents a cursory inspection and finds nothing untoward. In fact, the opposite is true. We owe a huge debt of gratitude to Mother, for it contains clothes she has made for my boys and Jane's girls. This will please Matron no end, as gifts like this help to save the cost and the time we women spend making and mending the workhouse uniforms and spare clothes.

*

After another arduous day of ceaseless floor scrubbing, laundry, and making enormous pots of soup, I'm done in. I'm more than ready for a short rest with Jane after our bread and vegetable soup supper, savouring the last few minutes before preparing the children for bed.

I am eager to share the welcome news.

"Mother has left us a parcel, Jane; I collected it from the office. She's generously sewn some extra clothes for the children. Of course, Matron insisted on giving it a quick inspection, but she found nothing to concern her, thank the Lord. In fact, she had every reason to be delighted; more expense saved for the house."

I show Jane the bulging brown paper parcel and we unpack it together. We save the string, fold up the paper to hand over to Matron, and we inspect the clothes – intended for 'Sunday best occasions' – warm trousers, gloves, mufflers and thick shirts, each one knitted or sewn by Mother's fair hand. It wouldn't surprise me if she had cut down on her food in order to afford the wool and the materials.

Jane is in high spirits. "This is indeed a generous thought; your mother is very kind."

And … there is a secret.

Carefully hidden in the spacious pockets of the trousers and tucked into the mufflers and in the fingers of the gloves, we discover tiny parcels of bluebell bulbs. And folded into the shirt cuffs and pockets are clusters of wildflower seeds, in twists of paper safely secured with twine

Thank goodness Matron had only given the contents a cursory search.

I have always adored bluebells. When I was a child, Mother taught me about wildflowers and their meanings. She told me that you give someone a bunch of bluebells when you want to show your gratitude, and gratitude to Mother is certainly what we feel today.

Mother – and not Matron – has had the last word. Now we'll be able to grow some flowers to cheer the bleak yard and add colour to our plain parlours, despite Matron's disapproval.

I will appear suitably bewildered and amazed when they *unexpectedly* bloom outside our door.

Chapter 40

Something appalling ...

Susie
March 2019

Sleep won't come. Again.

It has become more and more elusive since the move and all the mysterious goings on. I lie still, staring up at the ceiling. I'd decided not to tell Steve what Kate and Graham said about the whole Ellen situation, I can't face any more criticism. He's snoring beside me, oblivious to my wakefulness.

I wander downstairs to make a mug of sleep-inducing hot chocolate, accidentally finding some naughty chocolate digestives to comfort myself with. I sit up in bed to read.

While I'm reading, I look up from my book, disturbed by the – no longer surprising – insistent ticking from downstairs. There is an eerie, yet familiar, change of atmosphere in the bedroom. It's darker, colder and gloomier. My bedside lamp has almost dimmed to nothing, and if I look out of the window, I know there'll be no sign of the lawn, flower borders or trees.

Only the barren workhouse yard.

Defeated by the lack of light, I put down my book, take off my reading glasses and start to shiver. *I* know why it is chilly, but Steve will simply say the heating has gone off.

As my eyes adjust to the gloom, I'm startled and, I have to admit, a bit scared, to discover that Ellen is right *here*, in the bedroom, close enough for me to reach over and touch her. But I know I mustn't. My eyes widen and I stay perfectly still. This is the first time she and I have been so near to one another, and I'm utterly overcome. In the semi-darkness I can make out her shape, as she stands in front of the window, trembling, in her thin white workhouse nightdress.

She stares forlornly down into the yard before she slowly turns around. Tears are streaming down her cheeks. She covers her face with her hands, before giving way and sinking down on the window seat. I long to comfort her with a cuddle, but I know I must leave her be.

She sobs.

As ever, I can hear no sound, but her whole body is shaking. This is *sorrow* – like I've never seen it before. Sorrow isn't a word we often use nowadays, but it sums up the emotion I'm sharing with Ellen tonight.

She has no fight left, no strength to cope.

She needs my help, more than ever.

This is clearly the result of something tragic, far worse than her miserable workhouse life.

I don't move – willing her to stay – but I suspect she will leave. She pulls herself to her feet and drifts the few steps towards the open bedroom door. I carefully pull back the bedclothes, ready to follow her.

I wait on the landing for several seconds, in case I should scare her, if by any chance she can see me, before I follow her down the stairs. I watch her huddle close to the dying fire, before she wraps her arms around herself for comfort, in her wooden armchair.

I can't help it, my tears join in with hers.

Mittens comes trotting in from the kitchen, looking for a fuss, and jumps up on her lap, kneading intently with her paws, her powerful, protective purr joining in with the ominous ticking of the grandfather clock.

Back in our bedroom, while Steve snores, I make myself as comfortable as I can on the window seat, struggling to puzzle out how I will ever be able to help Ellen out of her misery.

A sudden movement in the gloom of the yard catches my eye and my cheeks are wet once again as I watch, transfixed, as a solitary, menacing magpie takes off from the workhouse wall.

Chapter 41

'One for sorrow'

Ellen
March 1881

The moment I wake on this mournful morning, a feeling of foreboding grips me. The feeling only deepens when I spot a magpie perched on the yard wall. A grim omen if ever there was one. All country children know the old rhyme about magpies: "One for sorrow, two for joy". We used to search and search, with our fingers firmly crossed, until we found magpie number two and could uncross them, knowing we were safe from harm. I know it's foolish to follow superstitions, but I still do today, despite my head telling me it's foolish. That's what comes of being brought up in the country I suppose.

I'm scanning frantically around the yard, as I had in my childhood, over and over, watching for the second magpie to appear, to transform the threat of sorrow into the promise of joy – but in vain. An ominous disquiet haunts me throughout the morning while I carry out my burdensome duties.

I should be feeling cheery; the bluebell bulbs and the wildflower seeds had been a precious and unexpected gift. At her next visit, Mother will be excited to hear how I've discretely planted some of the bluebell bulbs by our outside door, as well as in the front of the vegetable patch, near the rubbish heap. Their glossy leaves will soon poke through the soil and, come late April, if we're still here, will reward us with their flowers and fragrance. I wonder what Matron will make of that.

I'm clearing away the tables, ready to wash the piles of dishes after our scant dinner of boiled fat bacon and potatoes, when I'm alarmed to see her bustling towards the kitchen from her office.

Her face is grim.

"Ellen dear," an endearment she rarely utters, "you must come quickly. Your mother has arrived. She looks stricken and I'm worried, as we weren't expecting her. This is not her regular visiting time."

My heart is in my mouth as I accompany Matron to the dreary, unwelcoming office, the image of the solitary magpie firmly established at the front of my mind. I take care to see that James is out of the way, in the children's tiny playroom with Jane's girls.

It's written all over Mother's face, no need for her to say a single word. She rushes towards me and wraps me in her comforting arms.

I whisper, "It's my Joe, isn't it …?"

We sob.

Matron tucks her handkerchief – already damp with tears – away in her apron pocket. "I'll leave you alone with your mother for a few minutes, Ellen." She withdraws from the office, leaving the door ajar, to listen discreetly outside.

Our tears flow.

Neither of us can speak.

Mother slowly shakes her head, her body slumped against mine.

My Joe has gone.

At long last, Mother finds her voice. "He'd secured a position, love, with a good wage, on a large farm up in the north of the county, near Alton."

I squeeze my eyes tight shut and grip her hand for fear I might faint.

"There was a dreadful accident. He was helping to repair some rotting roof thatch."

Has my heart ever thudded more loudly?

"He fell from a high ladder but..."

Deathly silence enshrouds us.

I bury my face in my hands, praying silently for my

torment to ease. But in vain.

"The farmer is distraught, love. He rode a day's journey to find me; he wanted to tell me in person, to let me know how much Joe would be missed. He'd only been working there a few weeks – sleeping on the farm – but was already living up to his reputation as a hard worker, and a credit to our family. They were going to keep him on. He brought me the few shillings Joe had earned. The poor man asked me to convey his sincere condolences to you and the boys."

The boys!

I shudder.

How can I tell this grievous news to James and Henry? That their loving father has left this world and will never be coming back? It won't take long for Henry to work it out – without me telling him – that our hopes of leaving the house are dashed.

And all for a few shillings.

I wrap my arms around myself for comfort.

Matron re-enters the room, clearly moved by what she's overheard. "This is indeed a dreadful occurrence, Ellen. You may cease your duties for the rest of the day, but I'll expect you back at your work at eight o'clock tomorrow morning. At supper-time prayers Master will ask God to keep you and your family in his loving care, at this sad time."

Mother rises to take her leave, thanking Matron for her understanding. I press my face into her softness for one final embrace, before she sets off on her solitary, sorrowful journey.

I stumble my way back to our cottage and go straight upstairs to the bedroom. I sink down on the comfortless flock mattress and hide my head under a blanket, to mask my bitter tears.

I am aware of nothing but the weight of my grief.

After an exhausted sleep, I rise from the bed to move closer to the window, looking down over the yard in the gathering gloom of the late afternoon, allowing my tears to tumble freely again. I sink down, despairing, on the wooden bench by the window and surrender to my sobs as if they will never cease.

I need help, like I've never needed it before; to find a way to leave this place, to go home. But without Joe's wages, what can we do? My planned work for the squire won't be sufficient to enable us to make ends meet. There's no point in pretending otherwise: we will remain in the house for the rest of our days.

Little by little, I summon my inner strength. Deep in my heart I know that my Joe would expect no less of me than to face my grief with courage and dignity. Despite his undeserved misfortune, and our desolation, I must never give up hope, even when it's slipping swiftly and cruelly out of my grasp.

I have no appetite for supper but Jane, James and the girls will soon be returning, and it will be time to prepare the young ones for bed. I must do my utmost to suppress my sorrow for tonight but will have to somehow find the heart to disclose the dreadful tidings to my boys in the morning.

I light the fire in readiness for their return and wash my tear-stained face in our metal basin of cold soapy water, in an effort to calm and control myself. I will give them no hint of what has taken place, until tomorrow.

Despite my efforts to disguise my misery, dear Jane detects my stricken mood. Without a word to me, she gathers James and the girls together upstairs, to hear them recite their prayers before settling them into their beds.

Once Jane has retired for the night and silence returns, I slowly climb the stairs to put on my nightgown. I slump on the wide bedroom windowsill, watching the children sleeping, while I cry silently for our loss. I can't imagine how to go on, knowing my Joe has gone. But very, very slowly, I manage to compose myself a little, to leave my selfish sobs behind, and I make my way downstairs, to be joined by my dear Paws.

Together we make ourselves as comfortable as we can

in the wooden armchair, staring into the dying fire, until I fall into a fitful, tearful sleep, lulled by the comfort of her purr.

In my dark dreams I tremble, while the menacing magpie spreads its wings, preparing to fly away from the workhouse wall, its woeful work done.

*

Telling our boys that their father has died must be the worst task I will ever have to face.

Matron kindly brings Henry over from the men's side before breakfast, and he sits himself down in the parlour, next to James. Jane disappears up to the bedroom so as not to intrude, while I frantically search for the right words, my whole body chilled to the bone.

But there are no 'right words' to find.

Henry's shoulders slump. "What's going on? Why has Matron brought me over here? We haven't had our breakfast yet!"

I take a breath and close my eyes, finally managing to speak. "I'm *so* sorry …" I hold the boys tight, so tight, never wanting to let them go. "I'm afraid it's … your father."

James eyes didn't leave my face. Henry focuses on nibbling a fingernail.

"He found work, skilled work, on a large farm, but …" their hands grip mine, "there was a dreadful accident."

They stare at me.

"He was thatching, and …"

No need for me to say anymore.

Henry holds on to his young brother, despite his own threatening tears, while James sobs as only a grief-stricken child can.

Henry asks, "Does this mean …?"

"Yes, love, I'm afraid it does."

"…we'll stay here *forever*?" His face is pale as he says the words he never thought he'd need to say.

James interrupts, "What about our Nellie? She's Father's favourite! And the chickens! Who will collect the eggs and feed them? He said he'd be back to keep an eye on them again, on Sundays at least. Grandma has enough to do without taking care of them, as well as doing all her washing and mangling."

I don't know the answer to his questions. All any of us can think about is the fact that my precious husband has left us, never to return.

We are on our own.

Chapter 42

One last chance

Susie
March 2019

What am I thinking?

Am I naïvely hoping for a miracle? That Steve will suddenly turn back into the man I used to know and love? I've given him every opportunity to be alongside me, to try to believe me when I tell him what I'm seeing, but all I get in return is stubbornness, scepticism and scorn.

And why is that?

Because he simply isn't privileged as I am. He has no choice but to remain in his self-absorbed, sterile world.

On his own …

My sensible side warns me that telling him any more about my experiences with Ellen is a waste of time, but I'm embarrassed to say that I'm about to give in. My softer side has persuaded me to give him one last chance.

Just one.

In our early days together, he had a tender heart. He was known for it. Couldn't bear to hear about cruelty to animals or children; he'd be amongst the first to donate to TV appeals to finance welfare projects. Now his tender-heartedness is in the past. He routinely hides it behind a mask of indifference, and the miscarriage has only made him more distant, convinced that caring for a child was never a role meant for him. He tells himself he isn't 'good' enough and, sadly, he believes it.

Steve has to hear it. All of it.

Once Ellen is asleep in her chair with Mittens, I come back upstairs and gave him a gentle nudge. He mutters incoherently but doesn't wake up. I nudge him harder, with more success.

"What on earth …? What's going on now?" He leans over to switch on his bedside lamp, but it doesn't respond. He huffs and puffs, fiddling with the switch. "What's the matter with the wretched thing? For goodness' sake, there's always something … what with the flippin' clock refusing to cooperate, now this won't switch on …" He's in a grumpy mood, which is understandable; it *is* the middle of the night after all.

I jump straight in with both feet. "Steve, I'm really sorry I woke you up, but there's something I have to tell you." I use my best classroom *'please listen to this, it's important'* voice. "And it's not only about Ellen."

He grunts.

"I need to tell you … about the clock."

He cuts in. "The *clock?* The clock downstairs? What on earth are you talking about?"

I struggle to speak as calmly as I can. I fear this isn't going to end well.

"The thing is … it's not broken anymore. It's been ticking. Loudly."

"*What?* That's ridiculous. It's *broken*, Susie. You know that as well as I do. It hasn't been repaired, so how can it possibly be *ticking*?"

"I know it sounds strange but every time I'm about to see Ellen, it starts. The pendulum is working. I've checked."

"Did you say this sounds *strange?* This is a whole lot more than *strange*, it's *bloody ridiculous.*"

He sounds out of breath. I've hardly ever heard him swear.

"Oh, Steve. Don't get angry. I'm not making any of this up. Why would I? I just want to tell you what's been going on."

He grunts again.

"I was as confused as you are, when I first heard it; it was so loud, and powerful, you couldn't miss it. Quite unlike its normal tick."

"Have you quite finished? It's no good, Susie. You're living in a totally different world from mine and I'm not going to join you. I'll stay exactly where I am, thank you very much – where the clock *isn't* ticking."

"No, I haven't finished."

I almost lose my nerve. I have to close my eyes, choose my words. "I've seen her again. This evening."

I clench my hands.

Steve is sitting up now, with the lamp on his lap, its wire dangling. "No, Susie, you haven't seen her! How many times do I have to tell you?" He snorts, as if he has the whole world's troubles to contend with, and carries on fiddling mindlessly with the lamp.

Too late to stop now.

"She was here, a few minutes ago, in our bedroom – except it wasn't *our* bedroom, it was hers."

His shoulders slump.

Silence.

"And now she's downstairs, asleep in her armchair by the fire, with Mittens curled up on her lap." As I hear myself say the words, I know I'm laying myself open more scorn. If only he could be there for me.

But is that what I want?

Steve shoves the lamp to one side, raising his voice, "Stop it, Susie! For heaven's sake! This is getting ridiculous." He grabs the torch from his bedside cupboard.

I try to speak calmly, "No, it's not ridiculous, it's true. The cottage started to feel unusually cold and it was dark outside, with no lights showing. I could hear the clock downstairs, which made me shiver even more. I had to put my book down – my lamp had stopped working, like yours has now."

He shakes his head as I go on. "She was standing over there, in front of the window, looking chilled in her thin white nightie, dampened by her tears, before she turned around and sank down on the window seat, silently sobbing her heart out. I wanted to comfort her. I've never witnessed sadness like it."

Steve raises his eyes to the ceiling.

I carry on, regardless. "Once her sobs had started to subside, she managed to stand up and drift out onto the landing. I waited for a few seconds so as not to scare her, before creeping downstairs to see what she'd do next, and there she was, settling down in her wooden armchair, in front of the dying fire, with Mittens on her lap."

Steve lets out a noisy burst of air. "This isn't funny, Susie. First of all, you've tried, and failed, to convince me you're seeing a *ghost* from the workhouse, in the garden – oops! sorry, I mean the *yard* – and you've watched her find stuff you've left for her. Now, on top of that, you're telling me that this *ghost* – who you've even given a *name* – is at this very moment sleeping in an ancient armchair in *our* cottage with *our* cat on her lap."

Undaunted, I continue. "Yes, Steve, that's precisely what I'm telling you. In fact, the more accurate truth is, we're sleeping in *her* cottage, at the moment. If you'd been awake, you'd have seen her, and if you look out of the window now, you'll see the workhouse yard, in near pitch darkness."

He pulls a pillow over his face. "I can't listen to much more of this, Susie, and I'm *not* going to look out of the window. It appears I'm not only living on a totally different planet from you, but worse than that, I'm living with a mad woman, who's in desperate need of psychiatric help."

I cut in. "No! I'll tell you who's in desperate need of help, it's Ellen! She was sobbing like I've never seen a person sob before. Ellen is the one who must get help, and I'm the one who's going to make sure she does."

A long, pin-drop silence.

Finally, I speak again. "I've tried to keep these sightings to myself, and I know I said I wouldn't keep bothering you, but please, now you're awake, if you won't look out of the window, can you trust me enough to at least take a look downstairs? What could be the harm in that?"

This is the moment I've been waiting for. He won't be able to argue once he sees what I've got to show him.

"Anything, *anything*, if it'll put an end to all this *ghost* business." He perches on the edge of the bed, trying to summon some energy, before stumbling over to the door.

A rising temper is fuelling his tone. "But you must promise me you'll settle down to some sort of normal life after we've sorted this out, once and for all."

Settle down to normal life? Why on earth would I want to do that? I have an extremely important job to do.

I pick up my phone, camera screen ready, before following him down the stairs, waiting for his reaction when he sees Ellen sleeping in her chair.

Yes, she's there; of course she is, and this is my chance to prove it. I pause on the bottom stair and lift up my phone.

Yes! It's done.

I hear him talking to Mittens, but before I can join him, he pushes past me to go back up the stairs.

I brace myself.

"Susie. Listen to me. There's no one down there. No one. Only Mittens, curled up on her chair, as usual."

I'm beside myself with frustration.

"No, Steve. *NO!* She's there! Sleeping. I can see her, on her chair. Look! The photo! On my phone!"

I hand it to him, watching his face.

He peers at it. "What am I supposed to be seeing, Susie? It's just a photo of our sitting room. What's so unusual about that?"

Tears tumble. I let them. Defeated. The battle of wills is over. I must accept the truth – he can't see Ellen.

And why is that?

Because I'm the only one of us who can travel in time.

He doesn't dare to put his arm around me. He knows if he does, I'll push him away. I've never felt so bereft. I don't bother to mention I haven't been to sleep yet, he won't be interested.

I lie down again, under the warmth of the duvet. His

breath soon comes evenly, while I stay wide awake, picturing Ellen, my real-life friend from the past, overwhelmed with sorrow, sleeping downstairs by the fire, with Mittens doing her best to comfort her.

But Steve can't see her.

And, in the silence, broken only by the powerful ticking, a long-hidden awareness is emerging from deep inside: *I'm ready. Ready to put a full stop at the end of my sentence.*

*

The next night, while I'm sitting by the fire after our meal and Steve has disappeared to the den, I hear Ellen singing softly to her youngest child, trying to soothe him to sleep with a lullaby.

There's something unique about a lullaby. You don't often hear the term nowadays, but I remember Grandma giving me a bedtime cuddle and singing one to me when I was young. Her voice was gentle and comforting.

The lullaby Ellen sang to her child spoke volumes.

Of course, I make the stupid mistake of mentioning it to Steve at breakfast the next morning and, of course, he refuses to discuss it. "Don't start on about that again, for God's sake. It's Joan's radio, you know that as well as I do."

But I'm not having any of it. I know *exactly* what it was.

I have to act. It's urgent. I must find a way to help Ellen leave the workhouse. I could hear in her voice how consumed she was with sorrow, due to something far more serious than the drudgery of her workhouse life. Her burden of sadness can be seen in the way she carries herself, her stricken expression, and now the sobbing and the soulful lullaby.

How can I ignore a friend who is suffering like this?

What would I do if Kate was troubled?

She and I would be there for one another come what

may – it's what friends are for – all she'd have to do would be to ask and I'd be there for her in a heartbeat. Why should it be any different with Ellen?

Her only hope of a life outside the house is to be able to show the guardians she is no longer destitute.

All *I* have to do, is fathom out how to make that happen.

Chapter 43

Springing to life

Ellen
March 1881

Matron is showing us as much compassion as she can muster.

In fact, everyone is remarkably charitable in these seemingly endless days following our cruel tragedy. Henry and James are treated to extra titbits at mealtimes; Matron manages to put aside slivers of fatty bacon, supposed *leftover* fragments of suet pudding and tiny extra portions of lard for their bread.

I must confess, I'm starting to feel a little less sorrowful myself. I try to keep a hold on my dream of going home, although, to be honest, I'm very much afraid it will never be a reality, despite my faith in my friendly benefactor and in little Paws.

The house it is, and the house it will remain.

Can it be that having Paws to care for is helping me cope with my grief? She has taken up permanent residence close to our cottage, spending a large part of her day dozing in her grassy spot, when the sun appears. Whenever my sadness threatens to overwhelm me, she arrives, apparently out of thin air, jumps up beside me and works her magic – for that's what it is.

She's my timeless friend.

She has become my shadow. Wherever I go, she goes. She has singled me out, a curious but welcome occurrence. She thrives on the food I contrive to leave for her. In fact, I can see she has gained some weight.

I sometimes think she is trying to entice me, trotting ahead on the path to show me something as I return to our cottage after supper.

I had feared Matron would see her. At first, I thought she could sense when Matron was in the vicinity and thus managed to avoid her. But Paws is showing no interest in any other inmates, or indeed, they in her. I watch them pass her by without a second glance, and she in turn keeps out of their way.

Paws is visible to me alone.

She is my secret companion.

She has travelled from the light, colourful world of my benefactor to be my ally and confidante. I can't explain it, in truth I doubt it can ever be explained. But it brings me great comfort to know they are both here for me, and whenever they visit my world, they ease my despair.

*

In the meantime, I am grateful for the chance to sharpen up my skills in the kitchen garden. Working there provides a glimmer of light flickering at the end of every otherwise dreary day. I am now ready to ask the Master to allow me special leave to enquire about gardening work up at Longmead House, if the longed-for day ever arrives when we can go home. I'll have to ask Matron to find me an extra outfit suitable for the visit, and no doubt she'll be quick to warn me to take proper care of it, reminding me it is not mine to keep.

I am aware it is an unusual request, and Matron might think he should refuse permission. When all is said and done, I am merely a woman; it is rare for women to be taken on in a gardening job, rather than in the customary position as a housemaid. However, he is a fair-minded man, treating us with as much kindness and humanity as his role allows. He didn't dismiss the idea when I mentioned it to him before Joe died, so I am confident he will bear in mind how much I have to bring to the post and will support my application.

I am delighted that our vegetable seedlings are

flourishing, our hard work is well under way – carrots, peas, turnips and swedes poking through. Matron manages an occasional furtive glance at the developing patch when she passes by on her rounds, sometimes lingering for a closer inspection. But she has yet to work out that some of the tiny plants are in fact flower seedlings. They'll bloom before too much longer, as if by accident, and I expect she'll assume that birds have dropped the seeds.

The guardians make several unannounced visits to inspect our work, and the Master informs us they are much impressed, in particular with Matron's unceasing attention to frugality in encouraging us with our vegetables. He tells us they are more than satisfied with the prospect of future benefits to the house, and it soon becomes clear that selling surplus produce at the weekly village market will raise a substantial sum.

I took a bit of a risk planting Mother's bulbs and seeds, but I'm determined to provide a touch of colour for the yard. Living in the house shouldn't stop us having the pleasure of seeing a few flowers bloom.

I wonder who else will enjoy the bluebells when they bloom in the grassy patch by our door, and amongst the vegetable plants. They might wait until next year – it was a bit late to plant them for this year – but what a glorious sight that will be. Every day I carefully inspect the ground, looking for young flowers to emerge, but I hope Matron remains ignorant of them or she'll make us dig them up. She is adamant about it – there are to be *no flowers*.

Whatever will she say when they're in bloom?

I long for that day but, as yet, they remain in waiting.

I wonder; will my benefactor see them?

Chapter 44

When God is ready

Ellen
August 1911

Can you begin to imagine how it felt to be trapped? I couldn't make everything better for my boys, however many sleepless nights I suffered. Seeing them cry, longing to return to Mother and our old home, haunted me day and night.

*

Ellen
March 1881

Creating the kitchen garden is growing very popular. The evenings are getting lighter and the days growing longer, enabling me to prepare well for my possible paid gardening work. But I can't deny it, in my heart of hearts I find it increasingly difficult to believe that day will ever arrive.

Little James speaks up on behalf of us all, "When can we leave the house, Grandma?" She can't hide her distress at her next visit, when he pleads with her to take us home. She appears increasingly wretched and worn out each time she comes. I know she longs for us to return to her, but she is well aware it is futile to hope.

James tries his hardest to persuade her. "If we can come home with you, Grandma, I'll be such a good boy. I'll only eat tiny portions and I'll help you turn the heavy handle on your mangle, to save you getting too tired."

She struggles to maintain a smile for her young

grandson, trying not to let him see her anguish. She cups her hands tenderly around his pale, pinched face, and speaks gently, "When God is ready, James, he will help you. Keep saying your prayers and he will listen."

By and by, around the bedtime hour, I hear his plaintive voice in the bedroom. I creep upstairs and pause outside the door.

My tears aren't far away as I listen. "Dear God, Grandma says if I ask you to help us, you will, when you're ready. Are you ready now? To help us go home? Please can we leave the house? *Please*? I wash my face and hands every day, like I should. Mother says I've been very useful – I help to empty our chamber pots, even when it makes me feel sick, and I try to do as I'm told."

Sadness seeps in.

He is whispering now. "Mother told me that if we had some money, Master and Matron would let us go home. Can we have a few pennies please? *Please?*"

I have no warm words of comfort to wrap him in. All I can do is clasp him to me, soothe him softly, add my heartfelt prayers to those of James, and hope God is listening.

Chapter 45

By accident?

Susie
March 2019

"Susie! What on earth are you doing?"

Steve isn't amused and I can't say I blame him, the bedroom looks chaotic. I've strewn the entire contents of our wardrobes and chests of drawers in piles all over our bed.

I'm getting ready. The time has come, to sort out my things, my head – and my heart.

I grin at him. "Oh, you know what I'm like, it's spring! Time for my seasonal declutter. I've got loads of clothes I hardly wear any more. These maternity clothes can go for a start, and a lot of my things from last year are far too big."

He closes his eyes and groans, dramatically. "So long as you don't expect me to join in your wretched decluttering."

"Of course not; you can leave it to me, you know I love having a good old sort out. I'm working my way through our cupboards and drawers to see what I can take to the charity shops."

I don't add that I'm going to declutter all his stuff too.

He snorts. "And then you'll have a good excuse to go shopping and fill them up again, I suppose."

It's so sad to hear him speak in this tone; there was a time when he'd encourage me to go shopping for clothes, sometimes coming with me.

I don't respond – what would be the point? That would have been the *old* me.

Once I start, I'm in my element, and it doesn't take

long to fill several black bin-liners.

What I don't expect, while going through my box of trinkets, is to accidentally come across something I haven't worn in a long while. I take it out of its velvet lined box, and as I do so, I catch the long-remembered fragrance of lily-of-the-valley perfume in the fabric.

My warning frisson is building, but in a good way. The longer I gaze at it the more I realise that this could be exactly what I've been searching for. This could provide the answer to Ellen's prayers.

I won't even try to explain to Steve what I intend to do with my unexpected find. He'd gone along with me leaving the soap and the snowdrops – well, sort of – but this? This is in a totally different league. He'll never agree that it could work, for a start; not in a million years. He'll point out there's no one out there to discover it, so why bother! He'll say I'm ill, insist I'm not to go any further with my nonsensical ideas, leaving things around for workhouse *ghosts* to find. And naturally he'll say it will come to nothing.

But I'm not having any of it – it will *not* come to nothing.

*

I bundle the bulging bin bags into the boot and set off for Winchester, once the school runs are over and the traffic has eased, a broad grin all over my face The hedges are brimming with new life, the fields are showing a sheen of green, catkins are dancing – spring is bursting out everywhere.

I park the car and head for the hospice charity shop to leave the bags. I hand them over, and after a quick rummage through the paperback shelves, I pay for my books, give the shop assistant a warm smile and close the door behind me.

I pause on the pavement for a few moments, to look back through the shop window, reflecting on what I am *really* leaving behind …

Now for the visit to talk to the dealers. I practically fly down the high street, my precious find safe in my bag.

Steve has his obsession with his computer and his music, but my main interest has always been bargain hunting at antique fairs and bric-a-brac shops. I've never been interested in rare antiques, but anything a bit unusual and affordable will catch my eye. I've bought various bits and pieces in this market over the years – patchwork, kitchenalia, jewellery and furniture – if the price was right. I'd haggled and haggled over the grandfather clock, finally persuading the friendly dealer to meet me halfway.

I've sold stuff too. Let's face it, market traders love a bargain as much as their customers do, but today isn't about anyone finding a bargain or haggling, today is about what the dealers can *tell* me, sharing their precious knowledge and expertise.

*

On the drive home there's a short, sharp shower, but as far as I'm concerned it can pour for the rest of the day, the whole week even. I sing along to the radio at the top of my voice, marvelling at what I've learnt and – more to the point – at what it could mean for Ellen.

Determined. Yes, that's how I feel, a new word to add to my growing confidence collection, but one I'm clinging on to … for the long-term.

Chapter 46

On the brink

Susie
March 2019

Mittens is waiting for me by the kitchen door and pours herself through the cat flap. I replenish her food bowl before filling the kettle for a welcome coffee – secretly wishing for a glass of wine to take the edge off my nerves – and I sit down to enjoy my hot drink, along with a decadent chocolate éclair.

Her grassy food patch is the perfect place for what I have in mind. In fact, she is the key player in my plan – I'm relying on her. I've watched her relationship with Ellen grow ever stronger over the last weeks. As soon as she arrives on the scene, Mittens appears, and they both head straight for her special spot on the edge of my vegetable garden.

I'm pleased I let the edges stay a bit long and straggly. I can't wait for the bluebells to appear, but it's a bit early yet. Loads of leaves are showing, but I must try to be patient until April arrives.

I wave to Ellen at the end of most days now, as a matter of course, while Steve remains in total ignorance of her presence. We no longer discuss it – we inhabit separate worlds.

I'm intrigued to watch the nightly transformation of the garden into the yard, always announced by the broken clock: the way the dusk merges into darkness, the non-functioning of the porch lamp and the emergence of gentle candlelight. Workhouse food smells mingle with the whiff of dampness and mildew from inmates' cottages, until the light of the twenty-first century returns and normal cooking smells from my kitchen take over.

I wish I could know what goes through Ellen's mind when she sees me. Is she able to accept that I have travelled from another *time?* Not an easy concept for any of us to take on, but surely impossible for *her* to grasp, in her era. I know superstitions and spooky tales were common back then, but the idea of travelling to another *time?* It would be so much simpler if I could *speak* to her, explain what is happening, but that isn't the way our relationship works. Sadly, we never hear one another's words; we simply wave and smile.

And that's all we need.

Perhaps she wonders if seeing me is simply a dream she'll wake up from. If that's the case, let's hope it's a reassuring dream. I wish I could tell her she *isn't* dreaming – tell her what she's seeing is *real.*

How distressing it is to watch her grow thinner, her clothes hanging loosely, her hair greasy and straggly, and she looks perpetually dog-tired after her long days of work. Nevertheless, she somehow manages to produce a few tasty morsels for Mittens from her apron pocket and she always takes the time to give her a fuss. She always looks up at my study window, giving me a smile and an ever more confident wave as time goes by.

*

It's been a warm day, despite the showers, filled with welcome bursts of warm spring sunshine. Steve and I sit at the garden table for a while before supper, with a prosecco and a beer. My appetite has left me, in spite of tempting aromas from the kitchen. My stomach feels knotted, as if I am waiting to take an exam, full of nervous anticipation, knowing I'm on the brink of fulfilling my role.

Will Ellen work out where this third gift has come from? Will she realise what it could mean for her? Or will she feel obliged to hand it over to Matron and lose all possibility of leaving the house?

Enormous butterflies tumble around in my chest while I enjoy my welcome wine.

Something makes me glance up, to see a solitary magpie flying down to perch in the holly tree, where its mate is patiently waiting.

Chapter 47

Out of the blue

Ellen
March 1881

The moment I wake, I sense something unusual in the air. Something ... out of the blue.

I feel strangely at peace, despite the ceaseless tasks waiting for my attention. I picture my Joe's handsome face every morning as soon as I open my eyes, and tears torment me as I remember our love-filled years together, our shared hopes and dreams. But today, for some unknown reason, my grief feels a little less overwhelming.

When the six o'clock rising bell sounds, we get dressed and tidy our beds before shuffling over to the day room before the sun appears, rubbing the sleep from our eyes. Nothing special is dished up for breakfast, nothing more than the customary thin, watery porridge, bread and lard, and weak tea. I salvage a crust for Paws, who eats whatever I bring her, never failing to purr her appreciation.

After breakfast, before I get down to my scrubbing duties, I take a quick glance at the bluebell leaves by the door. How they'll brighten the yard when they come into bloom.

*

It has been an unusually uplifting day. We are all weary, but in good humour, the gentle spring sunshine bringing out the best in each of us. My chores are finished, and our recreation time feels well deserved. The six o'clock supper-bell rings and we gather around the day room table to enjoy our morsels of cheese and bread, trying as ever not to wish for larger portions.

The sun is setting as I return to the cottage, and I linger on our doorstep to watch the glorious colours transforming the sky. Paws is waiting for me, as is her habit, soon rubbing her head urgently against my leg, but on this particular evening there is a magical, mysterious air about her.

Now she is sitting perfectly still in front of the emerging bluebell leaves, ears pricked, staring at them without blinking. I stoop to leave her food, and there – amongst the straggly grass by the cottage door – I am confronted by something utterly out of place.

I can hardly allow myself to trust my eyes. This is amazing to behold.

I instinctively take a few cautious steps back and lift my trembling hands to my face. Paws waits, motionless, her owl-like eyes watching me intently.

When all hope is gone, when all light is snuffed out, that's when it happens – a miracle. And Paws knows all about this particular one – she led me to find it – and I'm convinced she knows it could be life-changing.

"*Paws!* What's this? And what on earth is it doing *here*?"

She flicks an ear.

"One of the wealthy lady visitors from the estate must have dropped it during a visit. If she hears that I've found it, she'll be furious; she'll accuse me of theft and report me to Matron."

I glance discreetly around the yard for fear I might be attracting unwanted attention, but there is no one about. Everyone is indoors, doubtless getting ready to make use of the remaining minutes of daylight to enjoy their tasks in the kitchen garden.

I put out a trembling hand to pick up something which has no business to be there, something which, if anyone finds out that I have it, could cause me a deal of trouble. I am truly favoured to hold it in my hands. Yes, I am a pauper, but now, could this be my chance to leave poverty behind? I hide it in my freshly ironed handkerchief.

I instinctively raise my eyes to look up at our bedroom window, where I feel sure she'll be watching from behind the curtains, and I hold up my handkerchief parcel for her to see. My face flushes once again as I see those gay blue curtains – in our un-curtained room – fluttering in lively air from a brightly lit world; a world I am honoured to enter, a world that has generously sent my benefactor and my furry companion to help me. I continue to watch while the curtains fall back into place, at a window where no curtains should be.

Conflicting emotions muddle my mind.

My first feeling is disbelief – what I'm holding in my hand could *not* be meant for the likes of me. I hardly dare to unfold my handkerchief to properly inspect what I've found, with Paws' guidance. She is still rubbing against my legs, purring, encouraging me.

The second feeling grows more powerful: that it *is* meant for me – and the explanation is beyond question.

I tiptoe up the stairs to hide my precious find in my clothes basket under the bed. Before leaving the room, I stand motionless and close my eyes, taking several deep breaths to calm my thoughts, trying to understand the full meaning of what has just happened.

This unimaginable event shows me that my benefactor is well aware of my wretched situation. It shows me she has understood my desperate wish to leave this place, and that she knows if we are *ever* to have our freedom, we must come into money, and *she has miraculously provided the means.*

Something makes me look out across the yard again, and my eye is caught by a pair of majestic magpies wisely watching from the wall.

Chapter 48

A deserving recipient

Susie
March 2019

It's time.

I hurry upstairs to the bedroom and carefully draw back one of the curtains, feeling shaky with nerves. The warning tick of the clock tells me that what happens in the next few minutes will either work – or it won't. Ellen's future is out of my hands now; all I can do is watch and wait.

The garden darkens, no lights except the odd candle at a window, while Ellen and Mittens stroll down the path, Ellen looking pale and exhausted at the end of her day. I am so proud of the way Mittens has learnt to coax her, patting her leg with a paw, looking imploringly up into her face. And she is clearly up to scratch with her temptation skills this evening.

She stops by the edge of the long grass, exactly as I'd hoped, sniffing around for her food, while Ellen stoops to leave her the usual scraps. She looks somewhat wary, pausing to glance around the yard, checking there is no one about. She pulls out the food from her apron pocket and is about to put it down amongst the grass, when she instantly stands up again and takes a few shaky steps backwards. She covers her mouth with both hands. Mittens' ears flick back, listening to her say the words I am not privileged to hear.

After a few seconds Ellen moves forward again and tentatively picks up my gift. She looks as if she is going to put it straight back in its hiding place, but after a long, lingering pause she wraps it carefully in her handkerchief.

She looks up at me, cradling her present, lifting it in wonder, a rosy blush and a confident smile transforming her wan face. I return her smile through my tears, trying hard to absorb all I've witnessed, before letting the curtain drift back into place.

She hides my gift in her pocket, and remains motionless, as if reluctant to leave, before fading and fading into the darkness, until the gloom of the yard has faded too, with the porch light shining out over the lawn once more.

As I stay looking out of the window, reluctant to leave, I replay in my mind what I have just seen – a drama I have instigated, a rescue mission. There is nothing more I can do now except hope and pray she will be brave, use her initiative and set it all in motion.

The next part is down to Ellen.

*

Before I leave the bedroom to go downstairs, I hesitate. Something tells me I am not alone.

Someone is watching me.

Someone vital to my plan – my lovely Grandma.

My grandparents had always been very dear to me and I loved listening to their stories. Grandma particularly used to enjoy telling me about their wedding day, showing me the photo of her wearing her beautiful lace dress and carrying a long trailing bouquet of roses and lilies.

It was strange I would find the solution I was searching for 'by accident', or did Grandma arrange it?

I know what I think …

I go over to the chest of drawers to pick up the silver-framed photo of their wedding, which has always had pride of place. There she is, with her precious rose-gold locket nestling at the neck of her wedding-dress.

How amazed and touched she must have been when Granddad presented it to her on the morning of their wedding. She often spoke, with a shy blush, about how fortunate he'd been to come by it.

"Those were desperate times, Susie. After the Great War there were dreadful food shortages, and rationing took hold. Everyday life was hard. Many unemployed men had to resort to selling off their wives' jewellery – the little they had – and if they were really desperate, they'd even sell their wedding rings, to provide for their families."

I turn my own wedding ring around as I gaze at the photo and think again about those poor families.

"Granddad got a real bargain when one of his workmates offered to let him have the locket at such a reasonable price. He could never have afforded to buy it for full price in a jeweller's shop. Mind you, he wasn't proud of the way he came by it. He consoled himself with the knowledge that he was helping out his friend, which of course he was."

How shameful it must've been for those men to go to their wives and beg for help, asking them to give up their valuables to be sold. And more so for the war widows, struggling to feed their children with no husband's wages. That appalling war had a lot to answer for; loving husbands never coming home from the battlefields, leaving their children to grow up without their father, or coming back wounded, never able to work again.

I speak to her photo, out loud, in the empty room. "Were you watching, Grandma? Did you see what happened outside?"

I swear she gives me a cheeky wink.

"What do you think? Have I done the right thing? I was thrilled when you gave me your beloved locket, your beautiful gift of love from Granddad. I felt extra special whenever I wore it. It was perfect for your wedding, wasn't it?"

Grandma's eyes are glistening.

"And you know how much I love the velvet box it came in. It still holds the scent of your lily-of-the-valley perfume, after all these years. Whenever I close my eyes and hold the box to my nose, I picture you, sitting in your comfy old armchair, in front of the fire, specs on, ready to read me a story, when I came to your house after school for tea. Granddad would be out in the scullery, sleeves rolled up, having a cold-water wash after his arduous engine driving shift, before bringing in a treat for us – our favourites – bourbon biscuits."

Is that a knowing smile on Grandma's face?

"I hope you understand how much Ellen was desperate for our help. Without your gift to me, and now mine to her, she would never have the chance to leave the workhouse. Granddad helped his friend's family make ends meet after the war by buying it, and now it *might* provide the means for Ellen to find her freedom and help support *her* family – all thanks to your generosity."

I smile to myself, imagining her beaming and nodding. I know how proud and delighted she would feel, knowing that Granddad's gift of love had passed to such a deserving recipient.

Chapter 49

My precious calico bag

Ellen
March 1881

It's no good.

I can't concentrate. There will never be a more significant day in my life than this.

I struggle to turn the cumbersome mangle, over and over, in the hot, steamy laundry. Too many once-unthinkable thoughts scramble around in my head as I glare at the daunting pile of sopping wet sheets. Can I dare to trust that this relentless toil is coming to an end?

Jane is becoming increasingly inquisitive and on our way to supper her curiosity gets the better of her. "My dear, you are far cheerier today; is there some good news you wish to tell me?"

"Yes, there is indeed, but you must try to be patient with me. I can't confide in you yet, but you are my truest friend, and you'll be the first to hear my news, as soon as the time is right."

After supper I venture out into the darkened yard. I can clearly hear the friendly ticking from the office as I risk a glance up at the bedroom where I'm rewarded, once again, by the sight of those blue curtains at our window. I feel my benefactor's eyes on me, and I smile my shy smile, reserved solely for her. She responds with her reassuring wave.

Matron passes by on her way to the sick room but shows no sign of noticing anything out of the ordinary. Doubtless she's preoccupied with the chores piling up for her attention, and as ever she doesn't appear to notice the bluebell leaves.

Back in our bedroom, I take my bag from its hiding place under the bed and carefully examine its valuable contents again, in wonderment.

However will I manage to contain myself until Mother arrives for her visit tomorrow?

*

The following afternoon I hurry over to the office where Mother is waiting, looking drained and dead tired after her long journey.

She's brought a bundle of newspapers and a few well-thumbed books for the house. Matron soon takes charge of them. "We are very grateful to you, Mrs Freeborn. Reading material is always welcome for the recreation hour, particularly for our less able-bodied inmates. Once they have finished with the newspapers, we can use them in the privies. I'll take these over to the men's side in the first instance. I'll be but a moment."

Matron has come to trust Mother and me to be left alone for a short while during her visits of late, a more fortunate occurrence on this particular occasion than I could wish for. Excitement makes my pale cheeks glow once Matron has left us, and I can't wait to explain the miraculous source of our good fortune to Mother. Her eyes sparkle as she listens.

"I didn't know what to make of it, Mother! I bent down to feed Paws, and there it was, hidden amongst the bluebell leaves in the long grass in the front of the kitchen garden! I could tell she knew how important it is; in fact, she enticed me – not only to find the locket –but to look beyond the obvious and discover hidden secrets."

Mother smiles a tentative smile. "I don't know what to make of it either love, and no mistake."

Poor Mother. This must be almost more than she can cope with.

A curious benefactor, a colourful garden appearing where the yard should be and, to cap it all, enticement by a stray cat, to discover *a treasure* so valuable that it might bring about our release from shame and destitution. She must be wondering what on earth I will come up with next.

I explain further, "To tell you the truth, Mother, I thought perhaps one of the wealthy ladies from the Big House on the estate had dropped it during one of her charitable visits, and I was worried Matron would accuse me of theft if I was found with it."

Her eyes light up as she asks, "And you're honestly convinced it was left for you …" she gives me a chary look, "by … your *benefactor*?"

I take hold of her hand. "I have thought long and deeply about this, Mother, and yes, I am. She has travelled from a distant time and place to help us. And so has my little Paws."

She sighs. "Well, love, I hope I can play my part efficiently. You're entrusting me with your future; you know I won't let you down, if I can help it."

I put an encouraging hand on her arm before continuing. "When you walk into town, you'll easily find the premises along the street where the railway station is being built. You can't miss it, it's just past the cheese market."

I spell out her mission carefully, so she is quite clear about what she has to do.

"Don't let him fob you off with any old price; make sure you stand your ground until he gives you its true worth." All the practice Mother and I have had at haggling in the market will come into its own.

I see Matron is on her way back across the yard from the men's side so I hasten to finish explaining, in a whisper, "When it's time for you to take your leave today, simply pick up my calico bag and take it home with you. Once you're alone and able to unwrap the contents and see it for yourself, you'll understand how important your mission is. I know you have great powers of persuasion; I don't doubt for a minute that you'll achieve the best price you can."

Mother's eyes are dancing now, she's always relished a challenge, and her earlier exhaustion has miraculously left her. The importance of her mission is clear. The future lives of all our family rest on the outcome of this one task.

We exchange excited hugs before she hurries away – a renewed spring in her step – and I can see she's holding on very tightly to my now – *truly* precious – calico bag.

Can you look back over your life and choose one significant day?

A day when your life took off in a new direction?

That turned your world upside down?

My day is about to dawn. And our whole family's future rests on Mother playing her pivotal part.

Chapter 50

A Victorian gift of gratitude

Susie
April 2019

Seven o'clock.

I've been awake for hours. Steve has left for his meeting in London and will be home late.

Perfect.

In every way.

Mittens jumps up on the bed expecting her usual fuss, but this is very different from her normal performance: her eyes are wide, unblinking, gazing intensely into mine. She paws at my arm – over and over – until I put out a hand to stroke her head. Her purr grows louder. Something is up. Did Steve forget to put food in her bowl? No. This is far more urgent than simply her food.

I follow her in my pyjamas, as she scampers downstairs to the kitchen where I inspect her bowl, but she has plenty of food. She waits by the cat flap, hoping I will save her the trouble of using it by opening the kitchen door.

A loud, reassuring ticking fills the cottage.

And, as ever, there is no garden to see. I'm looking across the workhouse yard, at events I've witnessed countless times in my dreams, but today it is no dream. This is the day I never truly believed would arrive. And now it's here.

I take a long, deep breath and step outside onto the step. There is no way I'm going to miss a moment, even in my pyjamas.

My heart thuds in time with the triumphant tick of our clock as I watch Mittens trot down the yard, tail in the air, to where Ellen is waiting by the gates, with her boys. This is so special – it's the first time I've seen James and Henry. No drab workhouse uniforms for them. They are smartened up in their 'best clothes' for the occasion: caps, grey trousers, woollen shirts, brown knee-length socks and shiny new black boots. What could be a more important day for them than this one, when they'll be *free?*

Ellen ruffles Mittens' fur, and the cat rubs herself against the boys' legs. They bend down to her in delight, stroking her ears in the way she likes. They clearly know her well: she looks perfectly at home with them.

Oh, my goodness – such a large crowd of onlookers. I can't make them out very well, they are hidden in a soft, misty cloud. Are the Master and Matron amongst them? And Ellen's mother? Have some of the guardians come to watch them leave? I would have loved the chance to see them – no doubt they'd be quite different from how I've imagined.

Oh, my word. What an *honour* this is. *I am taking part in a documentary about a Victorian workhouse.* How many of us ever experience such a thing? To visit *the past*, in *the present* ...

I'm amazed at the change there is in my Ellen. Still thin and shadowy, but she looks much younger, her curls freshly washed and gleaming, her face shining. There is a good deal of hugging, and wiping away of tears, before she leaves the boys to carry on making a fuss of Mittens by the gates.

Why is she hurrying over to my door?

Can she be coming to say goodbye?

I scuttle indoors to watch from behind the kitchen curtain so as not to scare her if she knocks on the door, but there is no sound. I wait for a moment or two, before she drifts back to the gates, looking almost reluctant to say her goodbyes, and where her boys are fidgeting with excitement, overseen by Mittens.

At the last moment, she turns around, in my direction, and waves – confidently this time – her tears of happiness falling unashamedly, as are mine, before she fades and loses all colour. Followed by her boys, she drifts to where Mittens is patiently waiting by the gates, before merging into her own grainy black and white film.

Tears threaten again, as I hear our *broken clock* chime its timely farewell.

Mittens pads after them, the tip of her tail triumphantly twitching, her purr getting fainter. The iron gates close behind them, gently this time, while a pair of perceptive magpies oversee the proceedings from the workhouse wall.

Tears blur my vision. I can't move from this spot. I want to capture this scene, in each minute detail; to be able to play it over and over in my mind, long after these moments have passed. I remain behind the curtains, just in case, but there is no more to see. The grim yard is giving way to the light and colour of our garden once more.

And our clock is silent.

I cautiously open the door and can hardly believe what I find waiting for me. There, on the step, is the most bewitching bunch of bluebells I could ever hope to see.

Ellen's Victorian gift of gratitude.

I pick them up, hold them to my nose and slowly, so slowly, I begin to dance around the kitchen, my fresh tears gently watering the flowers.

*

When Steve comes home late tonight, he'll find his packed suitcases lined up outside the front door.

And, mysteriously, his key will not let him in.

Chapter 51

A timely farewell

Ellen
April 1881

Our long-awaited day has dawned.

None of us managed a wink of sleep, unable to stop thinking about what this day will bring. I keep pinching myself to make quite sure it isn't merely a dream:

We are leaving the house, we are returning to live with Mother, we are paupers no longer.

My benefactor has proved to be a godsend, providing the answer to our heartfelt prayers.

James has it all worked out. "Grandma was right, Mother. We said our prayers, and God listened. At last, we have some pennies, like I asked, and we can go home."

Mother had managed to keep a clear head and persisted with her task of haggling for the best price for the locket at the pawnbroker's. She'd arrived for an unscheduled visit, giddy with happiness, to bring me her good news, and she'd been delighted to be the one to inform Master and Matron of the unexpected change in our circumstances – but did not enlighten them as to where the money had come from. I wish I could have seen the expressions on their faces when she told them we would no longer be needing help from the house.

Jane and her girls are swiftly dressed and ready for breakfast, almost anticipating with pleasure the watery porridge, the dry bread and lard. My mouth waters at the prospect of enjoying Mother's meals once again.

The time of our departure is set for eight o'clock, when two guardians will arrive to supervise the return of our few belongings, given over for safekeeping when we were admitted.

I explain to Jane how I'd come upon the locket, but she can't grasp it. She is convinced there has to be some other explanation. "Are you telling me that you're no longer penniless because you received a valuable gift from ... someone ... *from another time?*" I nod, as she went on, "And your mother was able to pawn it? For a life-changing sum?"

I beam at her.

Her face is a picture. "I do sometimes wonder if the asylum might have been a more suitable place for you, Ellen! So many strange occurrences have come your way during your time with us in the house. Very strange indeed." She manages a mysterious smile.

Poor Jane. She is clearly concerned for my mental well-being and I can't convince her otherwise. She only has my word for the existence of my benefactor and little Paws, and my belief that they travel here from a different world from ours.

We gather inside the gates. How amiable Master and Matron look this morning. Their earlier questions about the reason for our improved financial situation are put to one side. Two guardians are in attendance, puffed up with cigar smoke and importance as usual, but genial nonetheless. At any rate, there will now be three empty places in the house, soon to be offered to other *deserving poor*.

Master and Matron wait, side by side, smiling at us, ready to drag open the gates. Matron places a kind hand on my shoulder. "Well, Ellen, this is a day your family will always be truly thankful for, and that's a fact."

Jane's eyes are filled with tears as she holds my hand in hers, trying her utmost not to show her sadness at losing us, only her happiness at our change of fortune. Her girls give James loving hugs and he blushes at their obvious affection. They will miss him, especially for his help with emptying their chamber pot ...

Henry tries, without success, to contain his excitement,

shaking hands with the men and boys who have been his captive companions these last months. I'm filled with pride at both my boys, all dressed up in their best clothes, made by Mother. She has arrived to accompany us on our poignant journey, positively bright-eyed with excitement, despite her early start.

But before passing through the gates for the final time, there is one last task for me to carry out.

As I approach the bluebells by the cottage door time shifts, as I knew it would – signalled by a triumphant ticking from the office – and I am no longer in the workhouse yard. I am walking across a green lawn, past flourishing spring flowers, a sundial and a holly tree, to a patch of bluebells by her cottage door.

I am travelling to a distant world, a world of uncommon happenings, where at night-time blazing lights appear at the window, bright as day, where luxury soap is plentiful, where distant rumbles and roars from the lanes and the sky fill me with curiosity and wonder, where strangers become friends and lives are transformed.

How blessed am I.

Despite my efforts to keep them at bay, I'm shedding tears again, for the friends I am leaving behind. For dearest Sarah, who will doubtless see out her days in the house with dignity and pride, for Jane and her girls, who will inevitably suffer the same fate, and for each inmate devoted to the kitchen garden.

Lastly, I cry for Master and Matron, who have no choice but to remain working in the house for the rest of their lives.

I know my benefactor will be watching from her window. I hope she'll understand the full meaning of the gift I am leaving for her. I walk over to leave it on her doorstep, trying to chase away the tears, and as I do so her garden fades away. The time has come for me to leave her world.

I give Paws a lingering fuss, before she darts ahead and squeezes through the railings, unnoticed by everyone except the boys and me. She waits patiently in the lane, ready to keep us company on our momentous journey to her new home.

I shake the Master's hand and am pleasantly surprised when Matron steps forward to give us each a hug. The boys wave to their friends, sad to leave them, but at the same time excited about the new life of freedom that waits for us, with Mother.

I pause, transfixed, as I hear, from over in the office, the clock chiming a timely farewell.

I gather up the small parcel of possessions Matron has stored for us, put them in my calico bag with my precious lavender soap, ready to set forth on our joyful journey – back along field paths, over stiles and through sunlit woods – a journey I'd hardly dared hope would ever take place but a journey that has come to pass, because I have unveiled a truth, previously hidden from me: that there exists a distant world, in a distant time, beyond our ability to understand – but not beyond our ability to share.

*

Ellen
August 1911

Now my tale is told, and you have been an attentive reader of what might be thought of as an unbelievable story. But I can assure you every word of it is true, and I give thanks to God daily that I was able to experience such a unique series of events.

Can you accept that my benefactor travelled to me from a distant time?

Is it a strange notion?

Yes, it is – strange – but true.

Did it happen as I've remembered, clear as day?

Did I enter a distant world – where lights shine brightly, where colour and unfamiliar, mysterious sounds abound?

Did my benefactor travel from that far world to help me?

Yes, she did, because God answered our prayers. It was never His plan for us to remain in the house for ever.

We prayed – He listened – and our new lives began.

I'd like to say thank you to ...

David, Saskia, Josh and all the team at www.newgeneration-publishing.com for their time and skills. Without them my book would never have come out from hiding in my computer.

My son Chris – at www.retronaut.com – who kindly lent me his quote about living in the past.

My daughter Catherine who, as a Creative Writing tutor, inspired and encouraged me whenever I needed a boost.

My grandchildren Ruby and Zeb who always asked about how I was progressing with the story.

My writing friends – in particular Dai Henley – who encouraged me to 'get on and write it!'

My lovely friend Lorraine, Dai's wife, who, without realising it, gave me the idea for the title.

The Internet. It is impossible to mention here every helpful website I used but I must give special praise to Peter Higginbotham's site and his fascinating publications. You can find his work at http://www.workhouses.org

Reading about the lives of workhouse inmates in the 1880's was *almost* as exciting as travelling back in time. Now ... there's an idea ...